Deer Holiday

STEPHANIE FLYNN

Small Fish Publishing
USA

First edition
Cover design by Stephanie Flynn
ISBN ebook: 9781952372827
ISBN paperback: 9781952372834
ISBN hardcover: 9781952372841
ISBN large print paperback: 9781952372858

Also By Stephanie Flynn

Find my catalog at StephanieFlynn.com

Immortal Protector series

0.5 Vampire's Distraction

1 Vampire's Deception

2 Vampire's Secret

3 Vampire's Promise

3.5 Elf Bound

4 Vampire's Demand

5 Vampire's Destruction

6 Vampire's Conquest

Immortal Protector Side Tales

Deer Holiday

Love Claws
Depths of the Heart

Matchmaker in Time series
0.5 Minutes to Live
1 Seconds to Act
2 Hours to Arrive
3 Days to Hide
4 Years to Savor

Pirates in Time series
1 Pirate's Prize
2 Pirate's Treasure
3 Pirate's Plunder

Time Travel Romance Shorts
Fateful Time
One Crazy Time

If you like your urban fantasy without the romance, too, check out Stephanie Flynn's other name, Marie Flynn!

I

All Official and Fancy

Darby

CALL ME A GRUMP, but I couldn't think of a worse time of year than when humans flocked to the stores, full of spirit for the giving season...yeah, right. Expectations were the norm, not thoughtfulness. But humans were going to visit their families, exchange gifts, eat meals, and...hopefully tell embarrassing stories and laugh together. Every year new stories appeared, but old ones returned for new laughs. None of my old stories were funny, and I certainly didn't want anyone laughing at me. So, once again, I looked forward to another holiday with my best friend. Just her. Shauna and me, pajamas, a fluffy movie, and hot coffee with a blanket on my couch—or hers. We were neighbors, too.

I lifted my lips at the customer as she pushed her cart away, and I sighed as I started scanning the full belt for the next customer.

From the next register over, Shauna asked, "Everything okay over there?" She wore the same blue smock as me with dark jeans and a T-shirt hidden beneath. Her hair was pulled back in thick braids. I loved the eternal optimist, my neighbor, my best friend, but we couldn't be more different. Because of that, I couldn't fully open up to her. My world was hidden from humans. Had to be. Always and forever. That meant my small-sized fry was mostly empty of its fries.

Yeah, I was hungry.

But it was worse than that. So much worse, because of what I was...or more accurately, what I *wasn't*.

"Eager to get home. That's all," I said, a polite way of saying my feet ached. The store was a mess, and I'd been scanning items for hours, because all the self-checkouts were miles long and a half dozen of us had been called in to help. I didn't mind the extra hours, but I still couldn't afford college, and I didn't know what else to do with my life, anyway.

One thing was certain: I wasn't going back to my hometown. So here I was, collecting a check and trying to find my place in my very small, mostly empty fry world.

"Aren't we all eager to get out of here?" Shauna asked.

I glanced at the waiting line and swallowed back another sigh. We could go home if so many humans weren't so fixed on the *spirit*...

"Happy Holidays!" my annoyingly cheery customer said as she reached the terminal with her eager credit card in hand. "Sorry about all this stuff. I have a huge party to set up for, and it's so much work."

At her proclamation of a big, happy family, I gave her a fake smile and read off her total. "Sounds like fun."

"It will be, after it's all ready to impress." The customer laughed. "Well, have a good one."

"Thanks. You, too," I said the empty expected words.

Just Shauna and me.

The rest of the shift went the same way. Happy customers, hurried customers, busy customers still talking on their phones—one after the other until nearly closing. Finally, it was over until tomorrow. Shauna and I counted down our drawers and headed home together in my car. We could've walked back to our apartment complex, but when the weather was cold and snowy, and we left work in the dark, taking the car was safer. If I was going to get hit, I'd rather be in the car than outside of it. That wasn't pessimism. That was realism.

After parking in the surface lot, I held the complex door open for Shauna. Inside the narrow, carpeted lobby was a grid of mailboxes mounted to the wall. We both checked our mail. A curiously padded envelope had been crudely stuffed into my box. I hadn't ordered anything. It was probably the neighbor's package again. I flipped it over and checked the label, but it was addressed to me and from a law office. My heart pounded in my ears. I hated being in trouble, and official mail from an attorney had to be trouble.

"What's that?" Shauna asked, finding her mailbox empty.

"Not sure."

The law office's address was near my hometown—even worse news. I tore into it and freed a letter from a successor trustee, all official and fancy. I read it three times over before I could absorb the information, all the while pretty sure my heart either stopped or it pounded so hard, I couldn't hear it anymore. I placed a hand on my forehead and dropped into the lobby chair.

"What's wrong?" Shauna crouched down in front of me, hands on my lap, worry creasing her brow.

"They're gone." My eyes glazed over, staring at nothing while images of those big, happy families laughing at old stories and new ones flooded my head. The possibility of regaining what I lost had hung in the back of my mind, something to treasure, hold on to, a piece of myself. I didn't realize how badly I missed all that until now, because it was gone forever.

"What? Who's gone?"

"Why didn't they tell me?" I asked no one but myself. I knew the answer. I'd fled. I changed my number and never looked back. Attorneys had to track me down to deliver the news.

Because of *him*. This was his fault. His stupid face filled my memory and I crinkled the paper.

"Tell you what? What's wrong, Darby? Talk to me," Shauna pleaded, worry growing by the moment.

"Nana and Gramps." I would never see them again.

Shauna tilted her head. "But Gramps died years ago. What's going on? Is it Nana?" Shauna pressed.

"Nana's been gone for months," I whispered in disbelief.

Shauna launched herself into my arms and squeezed. I let her, and I dropped the envelope, ignoring the metallic clink.

"I missed it." I never thought of ever returning to that small town, but knowing I'd missed Nana's funeral left me empty.

And very angry.

Oz

AFTER I ADMIRED THE new junction box I installed with pride, I returned the wire crimpers and drill to my toolbox. I straightened and stretched with a long sigh. Another job well-done, but my back was sore from the unfortunate angle to reach where the mouse had chewed to the bare wire. Winter brought out extra maintenance issues, and as much as I didn't want the people I cared about to stress over things they couldn't fix, I appreciated the work.

I was a handyman. A jack-of-all-trades, as they called it. I should've gone away to college like my brothers had. The golden boy of the family, Jasper Martin, became an urgent care physician, but he was gone the longest. Harvey finished community college, and now he was the village's best mechanic. No matter what I could've done or wanted to do, I couldn't leave home, and I couldn't imagine living in a city, even temporarily. This village, these people, this was my home. So when Rigg's called with an electrical problem, I was there, snowy weather or not.

And I happened to be very good in the snow.

"You got it!" Riggs's voice carried across the nearly empty bar. His overhead lighting glowed bright, all the flickers gone.

I lifted my toolbox and the resulting corpse by the tail and carried them over to Riggs. "I got this, too. Where do you want it?"

Riggs tilted his head at me in confusion. "Outside?"

I shrugged and moved to the door. I flung the toasted body out into the snowbank and took in the fresh air. Flakes of snow began to fall again. We'd already had a wet winter, and it had only just begun. But it was great for the cross-country ski trails. Our village needed the tourists—the restaurants, the bars, the...motels. Okay, one motel. Magic Powers Motel had been the shining beacon of our village, the classic holiday retreat in the winter, a family's delight in the summer, and the hunter's paradise in the fall. Ol' lady Nana had finally passed on, and no one was left to run it. Now it sat on the highway, easily ignored, decaying with time. Such a damned shame.

The sight truly pained me. Nana's memory deserved better than that, but I'd inquired about buying the place, and the stuffy attorney told me it was impossible. The motel slowly dying a preventable death while the town floundered without it was my fault. And every time I passed by the place on my trips through the woods hunting or tracking, the woman I'd lost returned to mind.

Entirely my fault.

"You're letting in the cold," Riggs said. "Were you born in a barn?"

The tired quip was meant to be answered, so I closed the door and returned to the bar for my tools. "I was, in fact."

Riggs rolled his eyes. "Want a drink, Oz?"

I glanced out the window. The weather was only getting worse. People would hunker down. The plows would be out. Businesses would close. And with everyone safely in their homes and archers easy to spot, I could stretch my legs and get some fresh air away from everyone.

"Just one," I said, lowering myself onto one of many empty stools.

I could allow myself a small buzz before setting off into the woods.

2

An Obligation

Darby

MY EYES WATERED, AND I blinked the tears back. As Shauna lowered me onto my own couch, I repeated in a whisper of disbelief, "I missed Nana's funeral."

I sunk into the cushions, but I didn't feel the weight lifting off my feet after a long shift at work. I should've checked in on her. A phone call. A letter. Something. The woman had been in her nineties. I should've expected this soon, but I honestly thought she'd live forever.

All those years ago, because of *him*, I had to leave. I'd worked hard to create a new life from nothing but the clothes on my back, the gas in my car, and a few necessities in boxes crammed in the trunk. Now I had Shauna at my side, a job in my pocket, and a full set of utensils in my own drawer of my own one-bedroom apartment.

With a leaky faucet, but that was neither here nor there.

And I'd moved on. I was free. I was...happy? I didn't know. I didn't have the time to think much about it, but because of *him*, I missed Nana's funeral, and I hated him for it. He took that from me. As if that burbling hatred wasn't enough to focus on, Nana sought to destroy what I'd built for myself here. While frustrated at her, too, realizing I'd never see her again brought the tears back.

I swiped them away.

Shauna sat next to me and glanced around my claustrophobic apartment as if searching for a distraction. "Honey, you need more wax melts in here—a seasonal pine scent or something." She paused and frowned. "Management still hasn't fixed that leak?"

I blanked on what she said, but the words slowly processed. "What? Oh, not yet. I could've done it myself by now, but it's against the lease, and I can't lose my security deposit."

"I don't know why you're willing," Shauna said, face scrunched. "Plumbing is not remotely appealing. Here, you dropped this by the mailboxes." Shauna handed me my open envelope. "Sounds like something special in there. After the bad news, you need a little pick-me-up."

"Special?" I faced my best friend. "Nana is ruining my life."

Shauna made a twirling motion with her fingers. "Rewind. How exactly is your grandmother, rest her soul, ruining your life?"

By forcing me to return. To face them. To face *him*. Without her for support. I didn't answer Shauna. I didn't need more questions about a world she couldn't be a part of. I dumped the envelope's contents into Shauna's palm, and the key ring jingled to a stop.

"What's this?" Shauna asked, eyes wide with anticipation.

"An obligation," I said, frustrated.

Shauna frowned. "I was expecting a car or a house or something. What does that mean? What is this?"

Why me? Why not my parents? They were retired and unlikely to accept, but still, they were around. Or my cousins? They could handle it. "It's a key to a motel filled with memories of chaotic family reunions, laughter, and an annual Christmas tree in the lobby by the crackling fireplace. It stood, like, twenty feet in the air. You know, vaulted ceilings. It was enormous to my younger self."

And *he* had been there.

Shauna set the keys aside and gripped my hands. "What are you telling me?"

"I inherited Nana and Gramps's motel back home."

Shauna released me and clapped with excitement. "That sounds wonderful! I'm picturing that fabulous Christmas tree with warm twinkling lights. Now they have to be white, none of that multi-colored crap. The tree needs to look like it came from a magazine, not a daycare. Especially popcorn garland and noodle ornaments. Seriously. I love kids, but a sense of taste, they have not." Despite myself, I chuckled. "And then s'mores in the fireplace...wait, you can do that, right? Or is it against a fire code or something? Tell me more about this life-changing gift where you don't have a leaking sink that reeks and a property manager who can't manage."

Not the word I would've used, but I admired her excitement. Shauna didn't understand the full gravity of the situation, and I couldn't tell her, because our hidden supernatural world had to remain hidden. All Supers followed the rule, except the one time I broke it, and now here I was. "I left for a reason, and I'm never going back, not even for a motel."

Shauna's enthusiasm waned. "Couldn't you make it work? The place sounds perfectly cozy. And honestly, anything has to be better than working retail."

I popped a brow at her. "You think smiling for cranky customers in the checkout lane is worse than scrubbing guests' toilets? Guests who travel and their systems don't agree with a change in cuisine?"

Shauna frowned at me. "You said you like plumbing."

"Not exactly. More like I'm capable, and I'm frustratingly annoyed at waiting." I could fix a leak. I could replace the flooring. I considered myself fairly handy, but I didn't do electrical wiring. That was my limit for both my abilities and comfort level.

"Then sell the place and pocket the cash," Shauna suggested. "You could use it for a down payment on a house—get out of these shoebox apartments. A blessing in disguise, but you have to let me be your roommate. Share the wealth, honey."

I smiled. "That's not an option."

"Why not? Come on, Darby. Such a buzzkill."

"Nana's will states I have to run the motel or gift it to a family member."

"Then who are you giving it to?"

The million-dollar question. "Owning...and running...a motel is very hard. It's all consuming. I'll have to find someone *willing* to take it. A cousin, maybe, but I doubt it. Last I heard, my cousin owns a liquor store."

"He or she's qualified," Shauna countered.

"And busy."

Shauna sat back, enthusiasm waning. "So you don't want it, but you don't see a way out of it?"

"And there's nothing up there," I added. Besides *him.*

"There's snow. So. Much. Snow," Shauna said. Perhaps she finally understood. "I think it would be fun. What harm is there in trying? Go. Get your ass out of this building. Quit that shit job of yours and make that motel shine."

Guess not.

Not one to give up, Shauna added, "I'll bring you lots of business. Hell, I might even work for you, but I ain't scrubbing no toilets."

Despite the situation, I chuckled. Shauna could always lighten my mood.

"I'm serious. There's got to be some cool stuff up there. Tourists, a picturesque winter landscape..."

"Eight months of the year," I countered.

"Peace and quiet. Outdoorsy guys..." Shauna continued dreamily.

"Roaring snowmobiles and wannabe lumberjacks."

Ignoring my attempt to show her reality, Shauna kept painting her imaginary fantasy. "Fireplaces in log cabins with sexy men bringing hot chocolate..."

"My ex." There, I said it. Shauna wouldn't quit until she fully understood, and now she did.

Shauna faced me. "Wait, who's this guy now? You never mentioned him."

"Well, he's not really an ex. We never got that far. More like friends that could've been." And now could never be.

Shauna grinned. "Second chances are the best."

"That was a long time ago, and I hate him now," I said.

"With that tease, you have to spill," Shauna said, excitement returning.

"It's a long, embarrassing little story I'd rather not repeat." I'd rather have a colonoscopy, truthfully.

"A little story? There was no theft, no vengeance, no murder?" Since when did Shauna have such a low bar?

I shook my head in the negative.

"Honey, you need to get back there. Make that motel sparkle and let that beefcake swoop in for the romantic rescue."

He wasn't a beefcake, in the best way. He was lean and strong from hard work and outdoor hobbies. The external packaging was never a problem. Me being drawn to it in the first place was. He and I could never be, simply because he was human, and I wasn't.

Oh, and I hated him.

"I'll think about it." Over my dead body.

Shauna patted my leg smugly, as if she'd won the argument. "I brought the wine. Are we watching Die Hard? It's the best Christmas movie ever."

She was right about that, but she was very wrong about the motel.

Darby

I PROMISED SHAUNA I would look at the motel before deciding what to do with it, but I'd already made up my mind the moment my eyes absorbed the lines on the legal notice. I was heading north to look for someone to take it off my hands, get shit-faced drunk, and then drive home when sober, never to see the village of Powers, Michigan, ever again.

Except the time it would take for said alcohol consumption to reach maximum effects and cleanly wear off, was not necessarily worth sticking around for. A night of wine with Shauna, safe in my own apartment, sounded better.

I wished my best friend could've come along, but she had to work, and it was for the better. I'd have to scope out relatives I could dump it on, while fending off Shauna's arguments, and her being there only put my life at risk. She was bound to notice something off about my family. So with me off work for the day and her busy, I thought no better time than now.

But I hadn't checked the weather.

No matter. I was built for winter even if I didn't like it, but the county's budget and my car had limits. The snow was falling faster than the plow could clear it. As long as I kept my tires in the tracks ahead of me, I'd be fine. The steering wheel shimmied as the tires fought me for half an hour, but I pushed forward to the lands beyond reliable cell signal, regular gas stations, fast food, or any apparent connecting roads.

It might as well been called Hell, Michigan, except there was already a Hell, Michigan, and I didn't want to confuse the tourists.

I was tired, my arms were sore, and I seriously regretted some of my life's choices right about now. I could've been home, hanging out with Shauna while the legal notice rested peacefully at the bottom of my circular file. Eventually, the decision to ignore the situation would bite me in the ass, but whatever the consequences could've been had to have been much better than this treacherous drive.

The heater blasted the windshield to stop the snow from freezing and obscuring my vision, but the wipers ineffectively brushed at the melt, causing it to refreeze at the corners and slowly build up. The drone of the tires on the snowy mess lulled me, and no one else was on the road, approaching behind me or coming from in front of me. I was alone out here. I couldn't turn around, literally, with these ruts in the snow, and even if I could, I was closer to the motel than civilization.

To stay awake, I pressed a button on my phone to skip to a more lively song when a dark flash leaped in front of my car. Out of instinct, I slammed on the brakes—bad idea—and fought the wheel to turn enough before pulverizing the moronic deer that just happened to visit the front of my vehicle of all the damned empty places on the road it could've chosen.

Damn it.

I ground my jaw, biting back swears and out-of-control angry thoughts at the situation, when I managed to navigate around the dumb thing. But just as I relaxed for a second, my wheels caught on the deep shoulder and my car ricocheted, pummeling the snowbank like a linebacker at the ninety-yard line.

Turning the wheel made no difference. The brakes did nothing on the slick fresh snow. I careened into the ditch and the only thing in front of my frosted windshield was a rapidly approaching tree.

No, no, shit no. I couldn't afford to fix my car, but more importantly, I couldn't afford medical bills—if I survived. At this speed, without an airbag, it wasn't likely. I never would've believed this was how I died, but no one knew when their end would come or how. And like this... lost, alone, buried by snow on my way back to the one place I avoided like the plague? I was sure irony danced around in there somewhere.

I wouldn't be found for a while. Someone—likely Shauna—needed to realize I was long overdue and decide I was missing and convince someone I needed help. That would take time. And then that someone needed the resources to look for me and somehow manage to find me. At that point, I would be a gruesome sight.

Maybe not if I was still frozen.

Regardless, that person was going to have a bad day because of me, and I didn't want that for them. With nothing else to do, I pumped the brakes and frantically tried steering the car away from sudden death anyway, but it was no use. The car hit a pine with a sickening crunch. Glass shattered. The dashboard crumpled, and I flew forward until the seatbelt bruisingly yanked me back.

My instincts told me to stay away from this town, and I should've listened.

And that was lights-out for me.

3

The Return

Oz

As I STROLLED THROUGH the woods, snow crunching under my feet, the winter storm had thickened to near white-out conditions. The archers would've given up their hunts, so I'd released a burst of parkour—forest style. In the process of clearing my buzz, I'd landed on the highway, and at the same time, I'd fully underestimated the stupidity of people. What were the odds some idiot car would be out in this blizzard? Apparently pretty good. Damned city tourists risking their necks for...what? Everything was closed, as it should be. Paralyzed with shock and still slowed with a buzz, I watched in horror as the car swerved around me, about to kiss a tree. There was nothing I could do to stop it.

Useless like this, I darted through the deepening snow, heading back for my clothes, and I shifted into my two-legged form. I scrambled to dress, but the heart-rending crunch reached my sensitive ears, and I paused. Someone was dead or dying because of me. I had to get back there now. With worry pumping my blood and exertion warming my muscles, I finished shaking out the snow from my clothes and getting dressed. My feet moved full steam until I returned. The nose of the vehicle, now an accordion shape, curled around the tree like a discarded wrapper blown by the wind. I couldn't see a deployed airbag. Regardless of the weather or the lack of car maintenance, the crash was entirely my fault.

I shouldn't have had that drink.

I wanted to head back to the bar where I'd parked my Jeep. I had tools to help peel the people from inside, and I could attempt a cell signal to call for help, but doing so like this would waste precious time. I trudged through the snow on two frustrating legs with my heart perched in my throat. I ripped the car door clean off the hinges. Eh, no one could tell it wasn't causal damage.

I was stronger than I looked, but that was because I wasn't human—a fact that ruined my life, and there was nothing I could do to fix it. She'd blocked my number, blocked my view of her socials, and I couldn't even track down an address. Darby Hanson had vanished.

And that, too, was my fault.

A long time ago, five years and one week ago exactly, I should've stopped pining for someone who would never return, which my brothers delighted in reminding me, but that was easier said than done. Every day since then, I *chose* to stop loving her, but it didn't work. My heart couldn't flip off whatever switch made me glow for Darby. There was something that drew me to her, and every day I wished I could see her once more, just one more chance to make it right.

I ducked into the crumpled driver's side and checked my victim. One female, approximately thirty years of age. Her dark hair was matted with blood and stuck to her face, and more blood formed a curtain down her cheek but beneath all that, hers was a face I could never forget. As if I'd been sucker-punched in the gut, I inhaled a quick breath.

"Darby?"

The woman I'd lost had returned, and of all things I could've done to her, wrecking her car was about the worst. I didn't know if there was a way back from this, but I was going to try.

I carefully tipped her face toward mine. "Darby?" I repeated, heart hammering in my ears.

Steam bellowed from the radiator, and suspicious noises came from the engine. I had to get her out of here. The dash was crumpled, as I'd expected from the view of the outside. I reached over and unbuckled her seat belt.

With her hair brushing against my shoulder, Darby groaned.

"It's going to be okay. Can you hear me?"

She didn't respond.

While I was that close and personal, I checked her legs and carefully shifted them to see if they were caught. One moved freely. The other didn't. An igniting sound came from the engine. I didn't have time to waste, and neither did she. "This might hurt a little, but I'm getting you out of here."

I scooped Darby into my arms and twisted to free that trapped foot. It didn't want to budge. Orange flames escaped the hood. She didn't have time. I gripped under her knee and pulled—not as hard as removing the door of her car, but hard enough. As her foot pulled free, I lost my balance, but I regained it before we both fell into the snow.

The rapidly deepening snow.

Darby and I were accustomed to the cold white stuff, but the smart dude on TV called this a hundred-year storm. The county didn't have snowmobile or UTV transport—the majority voters chose not to increase the budget for the tentative purchase, and the blustery winds and no visibility meant a helicopter was out of the question—if one could even get here. And none of that mattered, since I couldn't get us back to my Jeep to call for help.

Darby tilted her head. Her beautiful brown eyes fluttered open, and she squinted as a gust of wind blew icy snow in her face. "Oz?"

She was just a little banged up with some superficial cuts. Or that was what I told myself. We didn't have a choice but to hunker down and wait it out. I gave her a reassuring smile. "Hang on tight."

Her eyes closed again.

With Darby safely in my arms, I judged our time before the engine blew. I already hurt her worse than ever and destroyed her car. I could at least preserve some of her belongings. I leaned into the car and flung her purse around my neck. Her phone rested in a pile of glass by the windshield. I shook it off and pocketed it. Anything else of use in here? A padded envelope rested on the floorboard. Looked important. I folded it and tucked it into another pocket. "Brace yourself. Here we go."

I suspected she didn't hear me. I adjusted Darby's position in my arms, and her head fell against my chest. A swell of old feelings rushed back, but I couldn't think about that. I had to get her to safety, and she needed medical attention. I marched through the drifts and a loud pop came from the engine. Flames ate up the hood.

I had no idea how I was going to make all this up to her, but I would do anything because I needed answers.

Darby

I DREAMED I HEADED north and hit a tree trying to avoid a deer—a normal Michigan fear, and a very real possibility anytime behind the wheel. But what wasn't a normal part of the dream was Oz, appearing out of nowhere to rescue me. I didn't know what my subconscious was trying to tell me or how I felt about that. Cold air, almost wintry winds, chilled my bones, but a source of heat made me shiver. I was so tired, and I felt like I was going to fall off the edge of the bed every second. Yet, I remained. Something strong held me. I must've left a bedroom window open, and I was caught in the blankets. What kind of wine had Shauna brought this time? I didn't drink often enough to know my very minuscule limits. I fought to free myself, and finally I landed on a cold, hard surface. Pain in my hip spiked. With a flinch, my eyelids fluttered open, and I blinked away the blinding, blurred light throbbing my head.

I was most definitely not in bed. Those winds *were* wintry. The snow was real, and I remembered driving, but I didn't remember how I got on this bench—once padded, now frozen. I fought to sit up. My face hurt. My chest hurt. My ankle hurt. And my neck was starting to kill me. There were aches in places I didn't know existed. But that howling blizzard had me trying to hug my coat closer, and I blinked again, trying to clear the haze from my vision.

A rhythmic pounding in my head had me press a palm against my temple, and as the pain eased, I realized the pounding wasn't just me. A man stood near me, trying to smash in the front door with a hand on the knob and a hip thumping against it.

I recognized that door. I knew this bench. I glanced out at the parking lot, and my focus returned. The sign out front confirmed my belief. This was Nana's motel. This stranger, who dropped me on a frozen bench, was now trying to break into Nana's motel. What else did he do to me?

With fury drowning out the pain, I shouted against the breeze, "What are you doing? Stop it!"

The man, bundled in winter clothing, turned to face me. I recognized the scruff dusting his sexy jaw, those thin but angular lips, the deep-set pale eyes that almost glowed under just the right light, and strands of blond hair poking out around his knit hat. In one blink of an eye, I peeled back those five years. My heart thundered in my chest, and as the fury rose, the pain in my body eased.

"Oz, you're going to break the door!"

"Settle down. One or two good smacks, and I'll be through." He returned to his task, hip shifting for another thwack.

I needed to pawn this motel off on a family member. The task was difficult enough, but they weren't going to want it if the door was busted down in a blizzard. "I have a key." I padded my pockets but found nothing. Where was it? "The envelope! It's in my car." I looked back at the parking lot where Nana's sign had come into focus. I didn't remember seeing any cars, and I scanned the white area. Nope, no cars.

What the hell? I rose, but my balance floundered, and I almost fell down entirely, knees weak...no. My ankle was a mess. Oz was on me in a flash, and he gripped me tight, holding me steady. I took the weight off my ankle.

"I took an envelope from your car. It looked important. Too bad it wasn't marked 'Here's the key, dumbass'." Oz sent me a crooked, apologetic smile and slid my envelope out of his back pocket.

With a scowl, I fished out the key ring, and Oz took it. "Why, thank you." He grinned slyly and returned to the door and unlocked it with ease.

I growled. Oscar Martin could be the most frustrating man on the planet—both attractive and obnoxiously sweet. And sometimes, so much worse than that.

Oz returned to me with his arms open to carry me, as if I needed help walking ten steps. I swatted him away. "Don't touch me."

Oz raised his palms defensively and kept his distance, but that playful spark in his eye pissed me off. Turning my back on him, I took one step and stumbled. Apparently, my ankle refused any sort of weight. Guess I had to skip the Christmas cookies this year.

"Looks like you need a hand to me."

Didn't matter if I did. He'd already done enough damage just by being here, and I had to retain some measly scrap of dignity. "I can do it."

I hopped on one foot while holding myself steady against the side of the building, and slowly—not without a few close calls—I managed to get inside and collapse on a lobby armchair.

Oz settled my stuff on the floor next to me and returned to close the door, but it bounced back open.

I grumbled.

He tried again without success. "I'll fix it." He set off on a mission toward the back of the registration desk and through the darkened doorway to the kitchen. Oz clicked on the light switch, but no lights followed, and he flicked them off. No electricity.

No heat. I rubbed my arms. We were out of the wind, but it was cold in here—the broken door didn't help any. I took in the worn carpeting, dusty fireplace, lumpy couch, and dim, gloomy lobby. As if all the warm memories of this place had faded with time, this motel was nothing like the inviting and cozy place I'd described to Shauna. That made the decision to pawn this place off so much easier. Pots and pans rattled in the dark kitchen, and Oz returned with a wok. As I glared at Oz's tempting but infuriating jeans-clad backside—the sooner we got out of here, the better.

"What are you going to do with that?" I blew on my hands to heat them a little, completely baffled how a cast iron wok would help with the door situation.

"It's the heaviest thing I could find." Oz wedged it up against the door and admired his brilliant work. It held...for now. Satisfied, he brushed his hands off and said, "A temporary fix. Where are the tools?"

"I don't know. When I was younger, Nana and Gramps didn't exactly point out how this place ran, and I would glaze over when Gramps tried to talk about the boiler. Why would a teenager care about that stuff, anyway?"

Oz gave me a thoughtful look. "I would've."

There was something deeper in those words, and I didn't want to think about them.

I didn't want to think about Oz at all, but I was kind of...stuck with him for a short while. I cleared my throat. "Check in back. I'm sure you'll figure out something."

Oz headed off on a new mission, as if avoiding me as much as I wanted to avoid him. The motel was a wreck and needed a complete gut job to bring it up to modern standards. On top of that, it smelled musty, and who knew what condition the frozen pipes were in. I didn't even want to think about that.

The Magic Powers Motel had lost its magic, and I couldn't wait to get out of here.

4
Trapped

Oz

I HAD TO FIND what Nana and Gramps Hanson left behind and make do like a caveman survivalist. I could happily weather the storm just fine by myself, but I had someone to take care of, whether she wanted the help or not. Darby was a stubborn woman, but now that she was here, I had a chance to break through that bitter shell of hers. I was owed answers, and I wasn't letting her leave me until I got them.

That blizzard wanted to stroll right inside, so I hunted Gramps's old toolbox. Unlike Darby, I'd been listening when Gramps went on about the wiring and plumbing in this old motel. At the time, I wanted to impress Darby, and I would've given anything to have old

Gramps be *my* gramps. I would've adored this building, treated it like the precious baby it was, and I would've been proud to take care of it and make it shine. Darby had taken her family for granted, and I wondered if some of her bitterness was because she'd realized that too late.

But that didn't explain why she'd left.

With my cell phone flashlight, I dug around the kitchen—full of pots and pans, utensils, canned and boxed foods—all coated with more dust than a wood shop. What I needed wasn't here. I checked the equipment room next, looking for Gramps's toolbox, an antique, heavy duty metal box that lasted forever. Just like this place. The floors were dirty—remnants of loads of wood having been carted inside, used up, and the mess left behind. Blocks of clean-cut wood piled in the corner, likely project leftovers from Gramps's tinkering and endless repairs. I checked the dinged and nicked cabinets, which were filled with partially opened packages of things I had no use for, but under a utility sink, I found it. I dragged the thing of beauty out and settled it on the counter. Like opening a time capsule, I excitedly dug through the collection and found all the good stuff, a little rusty, but functional. They needed the right touch to get these stubborn old things back the way they belonged.

I rummaged around the project leftovers pile for a block of wood that could temporarily substitute for a proper repair, and I found a suitable piece. With everything I needed, I returned to the lobby.

Darby focused on her phone, frowning at the thing that surely wouldn't get a signal in this storm—rarely got a signal on a sunny day. In her years away, she'd forgotten what life was like out here.

"I was cursed the minute that storm warned me off, and I didn't listen."

Her rant was understandable. "I wouldn't call your return a curse."

"No? I'm useless like this." She pointed at her raised foot. "I need my ankle wrapped and something for the pain and swelling. And I don't even know the condition of my car, but I'm guessing it's not good."

"You're going to need a tow," I said evenly.

"Thanks for the amazing diagnostics," Darby said with thick sarcasm.

"And probably a new engine, but Harvey would be able to determine that for you. He's more amazing than me." I had to get in that self-deprecating dig. Despite knowing she must be in pain, her dismissiveness stung.

"A new engine?" Darby lowered her phone, and her tone was less rude and more terrified. Those dark eyes bore into me, but they weren't filled with what I wanted to see. "I expected a busted bumper, a bent axle, and maybe a cracked radiator, if I was unlucky. Why...why an engine?"

"It was on fire, and after I freed you from the driver's seat, it, uh, exploded."

"Exploded?" Darby whispered. "The car's not worth a new engine, and I can't afford to replace the whole car, either. How am I supposed to get home?"

I approached Darby and kneeled by her injured foot. I needed to regain her trust before I could dig into the depths of our past. "Darby, we grew up here. Remember when we first met?"

"I feel like I've always known you."

I was happy to remind her of the detail. "Sixth grade recess. I found you stuck in a snowbank."

Darby's eyes softened with the memory. "I jumped off the side of the bleachers because I lost a bet. My friends laughed instead of helping me get out."

I smiled with the warm memory. "I pulled you free and dove headfirst into the snowbank to fish out your boots. And I even cleaned them up for you. We've survived worse."

"That humiliation was worse than a broken car and a sprained ankle, or a concussion," she said quietly, remembering more about the bet than I knew. Her softness melted away, and the stubborn Darby returned. "Humiliation is worse than a lot of things."

Ignoring that, I straightened and leaned over her. "Can I borrow that?"

"What?"

I pointed at her phone.

"What for? I can't get a signal."

"I want to check your pupils to see if you have obvious signs of a concussion."

"And if I do? What then?"

In the midst of her irritability, she appeared completely alert. If Darby wouldn't cooperate, I couldn't make her.

I returned to the broken door. From the bottom of the toolbox, I found bent nails and various lengths of straight nails scattered loosely. I picked out a few that would suffice and hammered the block in place, allowing the door to function. I stood to admire a job well-done.

"You call that fixing?" Darby scowled at my eccentric patch job.

"It's good enough until I can get the proper materials, but you're free to do better."

Avoiding my offer, her attention returned to her phone, and she shook it with frustration. This wasn't the Darby I knew, but I would be patient. I was glad she was alive and conscious. Everything else could come with time.

I shrugged into my coat.

"Are you getting your Jeep?" she asked. I detected genuine concern in her tone, and I called that hope.

"It's too far away. Until the roads clear enough to drive it, we're stuck here."

"We're snowed in?"

"Looks that way. In the meantime, I'm going to check the propane tank, and if it's empty, I'm bringing in some wood from the stockpile. Unless you object. I don't want to step on any toes around here. This is your family's motel."

She eyed me thoughtfully and shivered. "Thanks."

I pushed my way out a side door, back into the blizzard, just so I could keep Darby warm until help could arrive. Unlike her, I wasn't in any hurry.

5

Tetanus

Darby

MY HEAD WAS FUZZY, and it ached. My ankle throbbed and was swelling by the minute. My car needed towing and replacing, which I couldn't afford, and now I was stuck in this backward no-traffic-light village. All because Nana chose to burden me with the one thing I didn't want. I had no cell signal to accomplish anything, and I was trapped with the one person I couldn't stand. Oz owed me a long-winded, carefully worded apology, but even that wouldn't be enough. Not after five years.

It was too late for that.

Perhaps he'd forgotten what he did, but considering he remembered my sixth-grade humiliation, I suspected he remembered his grievous error very clearly and was slowly working his way up to it. I wasn't going to help him. He was lucky I was semi-polite. He deserved worse. And sitting here was only making me stew in old feelings I didn't want. I hated to be useless.

While Oz tried to find us a heat source, I needed to do something. I stood with a wince, keeping most of my weight on my good foot, and I invented a hobble-hop to move into the kitchen. Nana kept the pantry stocked in case the roads went out, and she had a motel full of guests to feed. With the condition of the motel, most of it was likely expired, if edible at all. Neat rows of canned goods still lined the pantry, and I sorted through them for something edible while cold. Frigid baked beans would have to do, and Oz would have to deal. As for me, I'd eaten worse.

When in my shifted form, I essentially became that animal in full—including the diet—and my shifted form liked acorns and loved half-frozen carved pumpkins leftover from Halloween. Surviving in nature was easier, and one damaged leg was less troublesome on four legs than two. And if I shifted, the cold wouldn't bother me as much.

But being a shifter also came with downsides. I couldn't expose myself to a human. It was against the rules of the hidden supernatural world. So, I had to endure as a beat-up human.

Inside the pantry was a push broom. I flipped it upside down and rested the bristles under my arm and used the narrow wood handle as a crutch. As I set a pair of cans on the dusty countertop, heat hissed through the vents. I coughed at the dusty air, and my lips lifted. Oz got the furnace running, and now we wouldn't freeze, but that meant the propane stove would work, too. I searched the cabinets for a pot and placed one on the stove. In a perfect world, the pot would be washed, but toweled off and blown on would have to do. Then I hunted for matches or a lighter. As if I were that lucky.

The MacGyvered front door opened on a groaning scrape, and feet stomped. Oz returned.

"Darby?" he called from the lobby.

"In here."

Oz leaned against the doorframe with a grin that made my traitorous heart flutter. "Heat's on."

"Thank you, Captain Obvious." Perhaps I used a little too much sarcasm. I was excited about his success, but I was still angry with him.

"You shouldn't be on your feet. You're going to make it worse."

"Are you Dr. Jasper now?" Oz wasn't a physician like his brother, or a mechanic like the other, but I noticed things here and there popped out. Oz was a great listener. He absorbed, and he was a quick learner. Too bad his absorbing and learning came to a screeching halt when it came to women.

"Never. His ego is too big for his own head. Any luck with food?"

"I have no way to light the stove or open the cans."

Oz, the amazingly helpful guy, dug through all the drawers I'd already searched. He turned to the toolbox, rattled some metal, and lifted a hammer with a sly grin.

"Really? What do you plan to do with that?" I pictured a sledgehammer falling on a watermelon. The result would be nothing more than a sticky mess.

"Convince some cans to spill." Oz bounced his brows playfully. "C'mon, tell me you've never had to resort to creative means before."

"If the pop-top tab snaps off, then I resort to a manual can opener, and if that can't do the job, then the punch end of an old school bottle opener always did."

"So, that's a no?"

I pressed my lips thinly. "That hammer is the wrong color. I don't want tetanus."

"Well, I don't want to starve," he countered. "Take your pick." Oz held the hammer ready to fire on the top of the first can.

I could shift into my animal form and graze, even in the blizzard, although it would be challenging. But I couldn't let the human go hungry, though. With a grimace, I nodded.

The hammer landed—claw end into the can's lid. He peeled it back and clawed further. "Lunch is served," he said proudly.

"I'm sensing a story here."

Oz opened the second can with the same suave moves with a rusty hammer. "My brothers and I didn't have the same advantages, and let's just say I was left out of family events. Sometimes I had to make do with what I could find."

I studied Oz. Even though he was incredibly handsome, he was a handyman with no real career like his brothers. His family's favoritism hurt him worse than what he'd done to me. I had an issue that didn't need resolving—an apology would be nice—but his entire life had been thrown away. He was stuck in this two-bit village with no real career prospects and no family of his own, because of the mental damage his family had done, whether they realized it. I understood that much.

I thought I knew Jasper and Harvey. I couldn't picture them tormenting Oz, but what happened behind closed doors rarely became public. I had enough family drama of my own without siblings.

"Brothers can be a handful," I said generically.

Oz shot me a glance I couldn't read. "Got a match? I prefer my tetanus to be warmed."

"I didn't find any." As I thought over Oz's story, memories of him and his brothers attending our annual Christmas party brought the answer to mind. "Fireplace!" I shouted, a little too excited. "Gramps always lit a fire in the lobby by the Christmas tree. Nana clearly didn't purge and reorganize after

Gramps died. There has to be something still there."

I hobble-hopped on my makeshift crutch toward the door, but Oz intercepted me.

"You're lucky to be up and moving at all, but that isn't an approved medical device." He pointed at my broom. "Despite your endless sarcasm and continuous doubt, I prefer you conscious."

Anger furled in my gut. "I've done perfectly fine on my own for the last five years. I'm not going to sit around doing nothing."

Oz smiled. "I didn't say that." He grabbed my arm and ducked under it, supporting my weight. He leaned the rejected broom against the wall. "Let's go."

His head was inches from mine, and my heart pounded. Being nice didn't fix the past, and being this close didn't rewrite it. "This doesn't change anything."

"Change what?"

I wanted an apology. It was the least he could do, but denying he did anything wrong at all—that pissed me off. And he didn't deserve to know he affected me so. I swallowed back my anger with a cringe. "Never mind."

Oz took a step forward, and I hopped, using him as a crutch instead. In his defense, he was more comfortable than the broom bristles. "Can you keep up?"

I could hear the amusement in his voice. I frowned. "Of course I can."

Oz moved again, and I forced myself to keep up, regardless of any consequences to my ankle, hip, or head. I couldn't give him the satisfaction of thinking I needed him, that I was useless and weak. Whether the heat warming my body was exertion or anger, I didn't know, but I would definitely blame one of them.

Not Oz's body touching mine. Nope. Not going there.

Oz settled me on the couch facing the fireplace. Dust puffed up into my face, and I coughed. He smiled and moved to the mantle. After patting around the abandoned decorations—fake flowers, holiday greeting signs, and photographs—Oz found a pack of long matches. He held them up like a trophy. "We shall have warm tetanus yet tonight."

I laughed. Damn it, but I laughed, and I tried to cover my reaction with a clearing of my throat. The slightest tilt of Oz's head told me it didn't work.

At the side of the fireplace, Oz collected a dusty old newspaper, crumpled it up, snapped kindling, and tented some cordwood in a conical shape. "This is all as dry as an Arizona desert in July after a drought. It should burn easily. I guess this is a bad time to ask when the flue was last cleaned."

His guess was as good as mine. I shrugged.

Oz lit a match, and within moments, the fire was crackling away. "Now for a bowl of delicious tetanus. You stay put, and I'll bring it out. That's the doctor's order."

I was tired from the drive, sore from the accident, and my head was hurting worse. The comfortable couch hugged me like a filthy fleece blanket, and, staring at the fire, my eyes glazed over. I couldn't fight him if I wanted to.

A short while later, Oz approached with a pair of steaming bowls. Mister boy scout over here being amazing. Where was this guy five years ago?

6

Prison

Oz

I HANDED HER A bowl of hot baked beans, and taking a chance, I sat next to her on the couch. Darby swatted at the resulting cloud of dust and shivered with a chill. The furnace worked to heat this old building, but all these rooms and the vaulted ceiling of the lobby took time. At least we weren't sitting at freezing temperatures any longer. While Darby indulged in a bite, I shrugged out of my coat and rested it over her shoulders.

"Okay, just stop," Darby said, pushing my hand and offering away.

"You're hurt. Clearly, you're miserable. I'm only trying to help."

"Why?" she asked, face scrunched.

I spooned a bite of baked beans and swallowed. After fixing mouse damage in Riggs's wiring, having a drink on an empty stomach, and running through the snowy woods, I was starving. I could still eat like a gentleman, even if I felt more feral than that. I chewed painfully slowly, also to avoid the question.

"Why?" she repeated. "I want an answer. Is this an attempt at an apology?"

I raised my brows. "Apology? I don't have anything to apologize for. You owe *me* an explanation."

Darby scoffed and scooted over. "You're kidding me, right?"

I wasn't, but I didn't appreciate getting attacked, so I declined to answer that baiting question by turning the accusation back on her. "Why did you leave?"

Disbelief filled her face, and that stung once again. After all this time, I still wanted to see anything but that and pure anger in her beautiful eyes. "It's obvious, Oz."

"To me it's not." And it most certainly wasn't. I'd speculated plenty, replaying those events, trying to decipher what I'd missed or said wrong. But for Pete's sake, I hadn't the faintest why she'd left. In my head I rewrote those events with me saying the right thing and ending up with an enamored Darby Hanson in my arms, beaming at me with all the love in the world. Of course, Daydream Darby had been easier to please.

"I'm different from you. That's so damned obvious. Come on, Oz. I broke the rule—not just any rule—but *the* rule. The one rule of my...kind."

I understood the transgression, but that wasn't an excuse to run from the safety of her kind. In fact, her choice to run was the opposite of smart. If she'd stayed, we could've protected her. I would've protected her with my life.

I still would, even if I'd grumble about her ungratefulness along the way.

"You didn't give me a chance to explain."

With her bowl of beans half finished, Darby rose and held out a palm expectantly. "Give me your keys, Oz."

Keys for what?

Darby

THE INFURIATING HUMAN DIDN'T understand a damned thing. The rule I'd broken for him could've cost my life. I fled from him in humiliation, but I also fled to protect him. He didn't understand the gravity of what I'd done for *him*. But he had the audacity to expect a chance to explain his gut-rending, soul-shattering reaction.

If I were male, I'd shift and gore him with my antler right now. But we shifters lost our clothing if it wasn't removed ahead of time, and Oz already saw enough of me. In some fancy big-city circles, shifters had access to special material that stretched and became invisible with the shift. It was expensive as hell, and I didn't know anyone who could afford it.

"I want the keys to your Jeep." I urged him to give them up with a flick of my fingers.

"Why?"

I snorted in disbelief. "You have to ask me that?"

Oz rose, meeting my gaze and standing a little too close. "I already told you; the Jeep is too far away. I'd let you try if you weren't banged up from the car accident. But even if you reached the Jeep, it's pointless. This blizzard makes the roads impassable until Rusty can get through with the plow. Even on his best day, he isn't keeping up with this accumulation."

His answer made sense, except for one part. "Why is the Jeep too far away?"

"What?" Oz asked and took my empty bowl from me.

I lost my balance but collected myself with a hand on the couch's armrest. "I was on the highway for miles with not a single vehicle in sight. I swerved for an idiot deer in the road, so if the Jeep is too far away, how did you find me?"

Oz's face burned bright red. "I was in the area." With that suspicious answer, Oz headed into the kitchen with our bowls.

I wished I could get out of here. Nothing he could say would ever fix the past, and I had no patience to listen to his excuses, anyway.

"Darby?" he called from the kitchen.

I ignored him, trying to decide if I wanted to hobble over to the fire, return to the dusty couch, or find another way to escape this torture.

"Darby?" Oz called again, voice sounding worried. "Do you hear that?"

I perked up instantly. Maybe some higher power was taking pity on me. "The plow? Is it here?" I hobble-hopped over to the lobby's bay window, but it was blocked completely by snow drifts. "I can't see anything."

"In here."

Hope deflated, and I was annoyed. I hopped into the kitchen and reached for the broom. Before I could grip it, stagnant ice water sprayed me in the face. Out of instinct, I jumped back. The spark of utter and complete blinding pain in my ankle, coupled with literal blinding pain stinging my eyes, meant I screamed as I fell to the floor.

I squeezed my eyes shut, waiting for my eyeballs to thaw, and hoping I didn't contract some weird brain eating amoeba from the ancient water. My ankle throbbed all over again. Now my hip joined in the party.

I felt myself lifted off the floor by strong, familiar arms, and a fresh scent filled my nose. Memories of us laughing and flirting—before he found out what I was—rushed my brain in a moment's comfort. I brushed those thoughts away. That was a different time.

I blinked away the freezing water and found Oz carrying me into the lobby. "Oz, put me down."

"When I get you to the couch, I will. Don't bother fighting me or I'm going down with you."

Oz was confusing me, and he was making it worse by being nice. "This motel is bullshit. I should never have come back. I knew I shouldn't."

The handsome face with a lock of blond hair peeking through his hat filled my view. "Then why did you?"

"The letter from the attorney says I have to fix up this heap of junk and run it or find someone in the family willing to do it. Of course, Nana had to make it hard on me. I came up here to find a sucker. I would've just sold it."

Oz lowered me onto the couch and adjusted his stance for balance, accidentally bumping my leg, and my injured foot tapped the couch. But that was enough to reignite the burning pain. I didn't know how many more hits my ankle could take before it checked out and walked away on its own.

I hissed in pain.

"Oh, sorry. Don't move, and I mean it. I'll take care of the leak." Oz took off for the kitchen, and several swears floated over.

I sighed, and my head fell back against the couch. I focused on the howling wind and batter of icy snow against the windows, trying to ferret out the sound of a plow scraping down the road.

All I could hear was the spraying of water like an out-of-control hose. The motel had thawed. Apparently, Nana didn't have the pipes winterized when she'd closed up. If this place flooded, I'd never be able to afford to fix it, and no one in my family was dumb enough to take on the liability or crushing expense.

This motel was going to be my prison.

And my fellow inmate was the worst person possible.

Yippee ki-yay.

7

He's Wet

Darby

SECONDS TICKED BY WITH Oz grunting and the metal clanging of the toolbox. The backdrop of spraying water had my anxiety spiking to the point where my own pipes would burst. If only my foot and ankle weren't elephantine because of a stupid deer—I really shouldn't say that. One time, long ago, I adored the magnificent, elegant creatures. But just like people, some animals ranked a little lower on the intelligence scale. That scale I fully judged by the ability to survive. The deer on the road? Strictly a zero. Me? No matter how much Oz would scold me, I couldn't sit here and do nothing. I was a ten, through and through. Besides, my own livelihood depended on that leak stopping, and every extra gallon of water soaking into the floor set me back that much further, the shackles that much heavier.

I rose and hobble-hopped to the kitchen, this time with my hand raised defensively against the next ice bath the motel thought I needed. And since I didn't get a blast in the face, I grabbed the broom and positioned it under my arm.

Now I could do something, except what I found nearly paralyzed me. Oz was shirtless and glistening wet with ice water. I should've had second-hand chills for him, but instead, I was perfectly toasty watching the view. Feelings from long ago, that I still didn't want, tingled as strong arms reached under the double sink basins. Muscles in his back shifted as he cranked a wrench. "Stupid ass plastic. Whoever thought..." He grunted with his force on the wrench. "That was a smart idea..." Another grunt. "In the heart of extreme temperature changes..." Oz panted, and the flow stopped. "Is an absolute moron."

I hated to interrupt the view, but I had to ask, "Everything okay in here?"

Oz startled, knocking his head on the sink. He ducked out from underneath and rubbed his head. He rose, still very much half naked and slick. Blond curls dusted his chest. Nipples were firmly erect—not that I was looking. They were just there, on my way to look at the rusty wrench in his hand. His broad, wet, strong hand.

Aw, hell. Nothing about this was right.

"You belong on the couch." Oz's voice was gruff.

"You belong wearing clothes," I countered.

Oz looked at himself as if only now realizing he was half naked. "I dry faster this way. If you don't like it, don't look."

That was the first piece of advice he gave that was actually smart.

"Exactly," he said in satisfaction at my silent response. After a beat, he continued, "There's a crack in the hot water supply line just above the shut-off valve. It doesn't appear the water heater is on, because it would've warmed by now and made the job easier. Someone chose CPVC, and that means the shut-off valve is plastic, too. Ball valves are a joke. I had to gently coax the thing to turn off without snapping it. So, that's some good news."

"Is there more?" I asked with dread.

"This appears to be the only leak, but I'll have to check each guest room to be sure."

"I feel like there's a 'but' here." What he'd said so far sounded bad enough, but I wanted to be fully prepared for the situation at hand.

"Dusk is here, and the snow continues."

I followed his gaze out the window. There would be no way out of the front door and into the guest rooms—where beds were, where more possible leaks were. That was a problem for another day. I couldn't deal anymore tonight. "Where're we going to sleep?"

"There's a couch."

I wasn't sharing one beat-up, dusty couch with Oz. No way in hell. Despite pushing that impossibility away, an image of him more than half naked on top of me...sprung to mind. My gaze looked for something else that might've sprung. Then I looked at the wrench in his hands. None of this was helping. I cleared my throat and dug the motel's key ring out of my pocket. "This key might open Gramps and Nana's living quarters upstairs."

"You can have Nana's bed, and I'll take the couch. Easy." Oz bent to collect his shirt and a flush of heat tore through me. I wanted to pounce on him, but humans were much weaker than shifters.

I'd break him in half.

"Deal." I averted my gaze and headed for the stairs behind the kitchen, and those extra steep, old wood steps stretched before me into a darkened abyss. Well, I didn't think this through, but I could figure it out. I used the railing to pull myself up each step, hopping awkwardly and, at moments, losing my balance. I panted, and from now on I wouldn't take having four legs for granted. At the top, narrow landing, I jammed the key into the lock, ready for a break from Oz and his sexy half-nakedness.

I turned the key, but the key didn't obey. I frantically jiggled the lock, but it smiled and waved at me. With an eye roll and an exhausted exhale, I slumped down onto the stairs and leaned against the door. Why? Why was this happening? I knocked my head against the door repeatedly, as if that would pound the right answers into my head or magically open the door.

Either was fine by me.

"Darby?" Oz called from down the steps. "Everything okay?"

I fought back tears. No, nothing was okay. None of this was okay. I wanted to rid myself of this cesspool and go home. Most importantly, I needed to forget the sexy, body-flaunting man with whom I'd shared critical parts of myself, thereby risking my life, and instead of accepting me, he'd slammed the proverbial door in my face. I waited for a beat until I was sure my voice was strong. "Key doesn't work. Nana must've had a private key for their door."

"Makes sense. You don't want the guests to creep into your personal bedroom. What's that banging noise? Did it sound like raccoons to you or more like water?" Oz asked.

The fading light, reflecting off the snow in the windows behind him, outlined Oz with a halo. As if he was deserving of that, but at least he'd put on a shirt. And I sat up here, shrouded in darkness—a shadow, a disembodied voice. My cranky ankle reminded me I wasn't disembodied at all, but I tried to ignore its incessant grumbling and the occasional yelp. I was disembodied, damn it. "It's not water. It's nothing."

"Do you need help getting back down here?"

Damn it, Oz. Just stop. Stop trying to be nice, because that didn't fix anything. "Nope. I'm fine."

He might have stolen something from me long ago, but my pride remained mine. I could curl up on the landing here for a night. The last time I went camping on an air mattress, I couldn't walk for two days, and the narrow landing would be much worse. If I rolled the wrong way, I was going to have a no-good, very-bad day. Since my ability to walk had already been compromised, I rose with an aching hip and hopped back down, supporting myself with the railing. Which thankfully remained attached to the wall.

When I reached the soaking wet floor, Oz stood right there, waiting, a playful grin on his gorgeous face.

"What?" I asked.

"I have good news."

"I could use more of that."

"Come sit down, and I'll tell you." Oz removed my broom again and rested it back where it had been. His thick hand captured my arm, and he supported me with his broad shoulders. I didn't fight him.

He settled me on the armchair and dragged over a stool for my feet. Oz rested a first aid kit on the footrest. Great. I could wrap up and walk easier.

"From experience as a younger and dumber version of myself..." He paused long enough to judge my reaction. I was thoroughly listening, hanging on to every word. But when he opened the kit, I became suspicious. "And a few key points from my brother's endless lectures, I don't think your ankle's broken. After I wrap you up, it'll feel better, but you still can't put weight on it."

I couldn't take it anymore. I slid my feet over the edge, out of his reach. "Why are you doing this?"

"Your ankle needs help, and we're a long way from the clinic."

"You know what I mean."

Oz's smile slid away. "You think I would leave you here, all alone, to fend for yourself?"

Last time I opened up to this stupidly sexy human, I had to flee for breaking the one rule. I was humiliated and left very much alone. Then I missed Nana's funeral because of him. I had plenty of reasons to hate Oz, but I still wanted to hear him explain. Call it curiosity, call it masochism. I didn't know. "I can't think of anything different."

Taking the hint, Oz leaned back on his heels, hands on his thighs. He looked at the floor, collecting his thoughts. I braced myself for whatever he told me next. Oz couldn't hurt me like that anymore.

8
One Bed

Oz

I WOULD ALWAYS WAIT for Darby. I had for five years...and counting. But despite all my attempts to be helpful, she wasn't warming up to me. I had to tell her something, or I was going to lose her, and that wasn't an option. Since she must've been devastated when she'd opened up to me, my only choice was to open up to her—regardless of her reaction. And if she did what I'd done, then I deserved it.

"When you showed me what you are, you didn't give me time to respond."

The anger rolled off her in waves. Apparently, that was the wrong thing to say. "I didn't give *you* time to respond? I risked my life to show you a secret, and your face told me enough. You were horrified and disgusted...by *me*. That's not something a person ever forgets. It stays with you, follows you, nags you. I never forgot, Oz."

I never forgot either. I'd replayed that moment hundreds of times, wondering what I could've done differently. And yet, here I was, about to screw up again. "I was new to all this. The things I learned... I didn't know there were others..."

Darby frowned. "What do you mean by 'others'?"

Until Darby had shifted for me, I didn't know there were others...like me. I shrugged. "Other deer."

Darby deflated, all anger flushing away. "There aren't."

I tilted my head curiously. Now, who didn't know everything? "What about your family?"

She eyed me, as if debating telling me more. "If they knew what I was, the whole family would erupt in mass hysteria."

"They're human? That's not possible." The ability to shift was a genetic trait. All shifters went through a puberty of sorts, and as far as I was aware, the gene always activated.

"They're wolf shifters, and I'm a deer. Let that sink in for a moment." Darby's beautiful brown eyes bore into me, pleading with me to understand. Didn't take a genius to make the connection of predator and prey. I understood her fears more than she knew. It was so painfully obvious to me Darby and I were meant to be. How could I get her to see it, too?

"You know what I am, and I can't change what I become. This is me." I wouldn't change her for anything. "And you can't tell my family, either. Promise me, Oz. Promise me you won't tell them what I am."

Darby was ashamed and embarrassed of what animal she shifted into. She was terrified then and still now of how her family would react. This whole misunderstanding between us boiled down to one day. The same singular day that repeated in my head over and over, as I tried to discover where I'd gone wrong. So that someday, when I had a moment like this, I would say and do the right thing this time.

A second chance was so rare, but here it was.

Five years and one week ago, Darby had shifted for me. In my defense, I was male, and Darby was stunningly gorgeous. Shifters couldn't take their clothes with them through the change—they'd tear or fall off. Supposedly, there were fancy clothes that could, but I figured that was a rumor. When Darby showed me her deer side, something I adored more than anything in the world, I had been shocked—in the best way. And while I processed that information, the image of her completely naked filled my view, and I was blinded—not unlike a deer in the headlights.

Sure, make jokes. They had to originate somewhere, right?

I was never in love with her more than at that moment. Instead of giving me a second to regain my senses that she'd bowled over, she fled and vanished. If I would've said the right supportive thing in that moment, everything would've been different. We would've been different.

Instead of taking some of the responsibility for her impatience and fear, she blamed me entirely. And now I couldn't tell her the truth about her car crash. The truth of what I was. She'd only hate me more.

"I promise I won't." I gave her a gentle, understanding smile. "Can I wrap your ankle?"

With a small smile, Darby lifted her foot back onto the stool. I gently lifted her injured leg and positioned the stool so her foot hung over it, giving me complete access. I peeled off her sock, and my heart sank. She was bruised, swollen, and it had to be so painful. I'd done this to her, and I had to do whatever I could to make it right. I took the roll of elastic bandage out of the first aid kit.

"Hold your foot like this." I gently positioned her foot, and with the bandage in hand, I began wrapping with just the right amount of tension. No one had to be a doctor to figure this out, but I'd had enough sports injuries in my youth to have plenty of practice under my belt.

When I finished, I hooked the clasp shut. "How does that feel?"

Darby wiggled her foot. "Steady."

I was thrilled to have helped, and even more thrilled she didn't fight me this time. I playfully said, "On that note, we still have one problem left to fix."

Darby's brows tilted as if the day's events had already exhausted her beyond limits. "Just one?"

"We both need sleep, but there's still only one bed."

"You can have the couch for the night," Darby said. "I can sleep in this chair."

Gramps had inherited the armchair from his father, and Nana reupholstered it. I liked the chair just fine, but it wasn't as much for comfort as it was for looks, and I couldn't sleep on it. I didn't want her to, either.

"When I was helping Gramps, I discovered something very handy." With a sly grin, I rose and headed over to the couch, a convertible sleeper sofa. I pulled off the cushions, found the strap and lifted. The queen-sized mattress unfolded. It wasn't anything remotely close to luxury, but it was better than the floor or that armchair.

Besides, I could keep Darby close.

"We can both sleep on the couch. I promise not to bite." Unless she asked. In that case, I was a damned vampire.

"Are you sure about this, Oz?"

I spun in place, arms raised, to dramatically make my point. "Do you see any blankets around here? The furnace is hardly keeping us above freezing. We can keep each other warm."

Darby wasn't convinced.

I pushed the sleeper sofa over to the fireplace, and I tipped a few more pieces of cordwood onto the diminishing fire.

"I don't want to freeze," Darby said reluctantly.

"Good to know being near me is better than death."

That got me a beaming Darby smile. Now I needed to keep up this amazing momentum...for the next fifty years...if we survived our tetanus-loaded meals.

Whoever said I didn't like a challenge?

9
What Sleep?

Darby

THE FIRE CRACKLED SOFTLY. The furnace hissed through the vents, and dust danced around. My ankle felt mildly better, which I was grateful for. As I laid in bed, a queen sized, lumpy, uneven mattress, I did everything in my power to focus on inane things, but my breathing was uneven. The dull distractions weren't working. I had to focus on fixing my breathing instead. Deep breath in, deep breath out. Smooth and soft.

Thankfully, Oz was human, and he couldn't hear how he affected me so. But when I'd explained my family were wolf shifters, he wasn't nearly as shocked as when I'd shown him my deer side. I supposed visuals were harder to process than words.

All I could think about was Oscar Martin resting within arm's reach, his muscular back to me, with his coat draped over him like a blanket. The last time I'd seen him was right here—at the Hanson annual Christmas party at Magic Powers Motel. The name was tongue-in-cheek. Our village was named Powers, and "magic" fit the theme Nana was going for.

I didn't tell Shauna how magical that night had been. It was packed. For a village, I was certain everyone was in attendance. Holiday music piped through the surround sound. Murmurs of voices, punctuated with laughter, and the tinkling of the glass serving bowl—punch for the kids—filled the lobby with a warmth I hadn't felt since. The adults drank beer in red party cups, but no one lost control or became belligerent. Although we had plenty of drama quietly circulating, everyone respected the kids, some young enough to ride on their mothers' hips.

The massive Christmas tree was decorated in white lights with a broad star at the top. Shauna would've loved it. Nana had always said the North Star had power. As a shifter, I thought that meant we had more strength when the North Star was visible, but I never noticed any. I missed Nana's whimsy.

She'd also set out a spread of hors d'oeuvres, probably to soak up the excess alcohol, but also to keep the kids content. Everyone was more than content. Free food and beer? Didn't take a genius.

But the event was beautiful, classy, and memorable. Oz and his brothers had been there, as always, year after year. We were the same age, graduated from the same class. Our birthdays were only a couple weeks apart, and our families celebrated together some years.

I'd had a crush on the blond since we were teenagers in high school. We were friends—family friends—but humans and Supers didn't mix. My parents warned me to keep that part of me secret because in the past, wars had been fought over it. Many of our kind perished, and unlike humans, we didn't repeat our historical mistakes. For all those childhood years, I didn't want to ruin what we had or risk my life.

Wearing a cheesy sweater, since he'd lost a bet, Oz had glanced at me from across the lobby, Christmas tree lights sparkling in his eyes. He continued to smile and nod at the conversation around him, but those eyes of his were only for me. I knew this man—I trusted him—and I wanted to be with him.

That perfect night, I excused Oz from his group and brought him into an available motel room. That sparkle in his eye remained, glowing, excited, and I was certain I was doing the right thing...for us. I was certain he felt the same about me as I did about him.

"I want to show you something," I told him.

With his angular lips parted, he set his red cup on the microwave table. "Is that so?"

"But you have to promise you won't tell anyone."

The corner of his lips lifted. Oz didn't gossip. He never disrespected anyone. Outside of my parents and one of my friends—another family friend I hadn't seen in years—I didn't trust anyone with my secret.

"I promise I won't." The same words he'd just given me about keeping my secret from my parents.

"What I want to show you might be...different from what you're used to, but everything's okay."

"Your disclaimer is intriguing." Oz kept his distance as if wanting me but letting me run the show on my comfort level, and I appreciated that. I still did.

"I need you to stay quiet, okay? No yelling, screaming, or...laughing."

"Darby, whatever it is, you can trust me."

Oz was completely trustworthy.

I started to strip, and that look on Oz's face was unmistakable. I gestured to stop him from approaching. "Just watch."

Disappointment flickered on his face, but he listened, quietly, patiently watching.

When I was completely naked—underwear, bra, socks—everything, I didn't cover myself with my hands. I hadn't been shy. I was scared. I was about to do exactly what my parents always warned me against. I was about to break the one rule my hidden world had. I didn't know the consequences, and at that moment, for him, I didn't care.

Oz got an eyeful, and he stared, lips parted.

Now or never. With a few deep breaths, I shifted. From a buck-twenty soaking wet and vertical, I became a four-legged doe at a lean buck and a half. Oz scrambled back from me and bumped against the sink countertop. I supposed now my nose had been a bit too close to him, but Oz was an outdoorsy guy. He knew deer didn't bite—we were herbivores. Prey species.

I had done it. No going back down. My elongated ears repositioned, chasing the sounds of the party. My white tail swished. With my sensitive nose, I was able to pick up scents on Oz even he didn't know were still there. The soap on his hands, the beer on his breath, the shampoo mixed with gel in his hair, the fragrance of his laundry detergent still lingering on that hideous sweater. But beneath all that, there was Oz's smell.

The same smell that rushed me back to this party when Oz had carried me. But that was where the dream had ended. The look on Oz's face was clearly horror and disgust. I'd made a grave mistake. I'd exposed myself, risked my life, risked my family's lives, all to win over a human's heart.

I was destroyed. To minimize the damage and potentially blame the beer, I shifted back, fully naked once more. Without looking Oz in the face, I dressed and ran out the door, never to return to the party again. Never to see Gramps or Nana again. Never to return to Powers, Michigan. Until now.

Oz claimed I'd read him wrong, that he only needed time to process learning other deer shifters existed. His face, his heart-shattering body language, had been very wrong. I never forgave him for that. I had two solaces after that night. First, that nightmare had been in private, and two, he appeared to have kept my secret or my family would've blown up my phone before I'd changed the number.

Then and now, Oz was completely trustworthy.

And right now, Oz slumbered on his side, facing away from me. All I could picture was him soaking wet, half naked, with those hard nipples of his on that sculpted, dusted chest. Narrow waist. Thick wrench in his strong hands, and something that might've sprung. He had been handsome five years ago, but while I was away, he became irresistibly, impossibly sexy.

He'd rescued me from my crash. He'd taken care of me, even if I was ungrateful and unnecessarily harsh. Perhaps it was guilt making him deal with me or perhaps it was more. Perhaps, he still held those same feelings for me. If I moved one hand over and touched him, I would find out. The last five years could vanish. We could pick up right where we'd left off.

Could I put myself out there again, for him?

10
Real Meal

Darby

I WOKE UP, COMPLETELY uncertain how I managed some shut eye, and found Oz's side of the bed cold. A wave of disappointment rolled through me. Just when I thought there might still be a spark between us, had he left? I glanced at the bay window, and I couldn't see anything but bright light above a frustrating snowbank. His MacGyvered repair of the front door held, and since there wasn't any snow or water from the door having opened recently, I suspected he didn't leave that way. I rubbed my eyes and sat up with a yawn. Oz's coat fell off me and onto the floor. I leaned over and picked it up.

Fresh cordwood had been carefully placed in the fire, and that was when I heard it. Metal rattled in the kitchen. Pantry doors squeaked.

Clicks from the stove. He hadn't left. He was making breakfast. With a quick glance at the kitchen door, I slyly pulled the fabric up to my nose. This was the Oz I remembered. I exhaled.

And I shivered.

That furnace was too old to maintain this place anymore, and I didn't want Oz to freeze. I rose carefully and touched my injured toes to the floor for balance. I wished I had... Leaning against the armrest of the couch-daybed thing was the broom. I snorted and smiled to myself while I tucked the bristles under my arm.

The initial pain had receded, but the stiffness and soreness made me feel a century old. I shuffled with a few grunts and groans toward the kitchen. But I stopped short when my bandaged foot absorbed the brain-eating, amoeba-infested water. It was still shockingly cold. I'd have to take care of that before major damage happened, but I couldn't right now.

"You're up," Oz said, smiling and lifting the lid on a frying pan. Steam curled into the air. Music played on his cell phone. Considering we were literally trapped in here, he seemed to be adapting well. Maybe too well.

"Of course you'd be in here," I said. When our families celebrated Thanksgiving together, Oz would always be in the kitchen helping. My mother would shoo him out of the way, but she secretly liked the help. I wondered if that was some of the difficulties with his brothers—that they'd tease him for joining the women in the kitchen.

"People gotta eat," he said.

"Need a hand?"

After a thoughtful gaze, he beckoned me. "I could use some help stirring over here."

Liar, but I was willing to help. I was willing to get closer. I managed one hobbling shuffle on my broom before Oz rushed to my side. "Hold up. I don't need you slipping on the floor."

"I do feel a hundred years old," I said, coyly agreeing with him. "I don't want to double that with another trip smacking my hip."

Oz took his coat from me, and without letting me go, he awkwardly shrugged into it. "I tried to find towels to absorb the mess, but I literally couldn't find a single one."

"The rooms have fluffy bathroom towels, but we can't get into them."

"Didn't Nana keep spares to replace them each day or whenever guests wanted to swap them out?"

I glanced up the stairs with dread. "She has a dedicated closet upstairs."

"That's not very convenient."

"Gramps's utility room was supposed to be the linen closet, but Nana compromised."

"That doesn't make sense," Oz said, still holding me tightly.

"Sometimes a person did whatever was necessary for the ones they cared about, even at their own expense." I gazed at Oz thoughtfully. I wasn't talking about myself. I really meant Nana and Gramps. I did.

"Is that so?" Oz asked with a grin. "Then I'll go get those towels."

"Door's locked," I reminded him. "No key." I paused for a beat, trying to figure out what he planned to do. "And no kicking in the door."

"My repair held."

"For now."

Oz was amused. I liked him this way. Truthfully, he was usually pretty chipper, but he seemed in extra high spirits today.

"When I can get to the store, I'll do a proper repair."

I think I believed him. But Oz still didn't leave my side, and the food was sizzling something fierce. "How about that help?"

Oz craned his neck at the food as if having forgotten it. "On second thought, I don't want you slipping on this floor."

"And if you slip on this floor?" As if I was the only one capable of being a klutz.

"I have remarkable dexterity."

"Uh, huh. Sure." I rolled my eyes. If Oz hurt himself, then we would be in bigger trouble. The village only had one ambulance, and nothing was getting down the road yet. Wait a minute. The light shining through the kitchen window was bright, almost sunny bright. "The storm stopped."

"At some point in the middle of the night," Oz said.

"Didn't you sleep?"

"Someone had to keep the fire going." *Sometimes a person did whatever was necessary for the ones they cared about, even at their own expense.* I repeated to myself.

Beneath his simple statement of survival was a confession, and it took my breath away. "Oh, uh, thank you." But I was still starving, and

I couldn't listen to food rapidly going to waste. "I can help, you know, before that's burned."

Oz released me. "Only if you stay close." He moved back behind the stove and handed me the spatula.

I hobbled closer, totally okay with his rule. "I recognize this. What is it?"

"Hash. It's not eggs with ketchup, but I hope it's edible. Over here, I have peaches and more baked beans."

"I prefer bones of my enemies, but meat and potatoes are a close second." While Oz gave me a contained smile, I leaned over the burners, taking in a deep whiff. I didn't know he still remembered my favorite breakfast. But after yesterday's baked beans, I was nearly starving. My deer side couldn't digest meat, but my human side? Bring on the cow. With a fork. I wasn't an animal...all the time. "I look forward to tetanus."

Oz chuckled. "Sorry to disappoint, but I found a real can opener, and it's surely tetanus-free."

"No more hammer?"

"Not today."

"It all smells great," I said, standing shoulder to shoulder with Oz. Warm memories surfaced again. "Last time we did this was Thanksgiving."

"Five years ago," he added. "You made the best stuffing I've ever had."

"And you made the perfect gravy," I said. His gravy, from scratch using the turkey drippings, was perfectly filling and lump-free. "I've never had better gravy. Seriously. In my whole life, Oscar Martin's gravy is simply the best."

"Thank you." Oz grinned, and a spark of heat tore through me. "Although this isn't going to compare to that."

"You can't work magic with expired canned food?" I asked playfully.

"Actually, I was going to say this was going to be better." Oz lifted a spoon of hash and offered it to me.

I leaned close, eyes locked on his. My heart rate jumped again, but I couldn't focus on my breathing. I could only stare into those pale eyes that almost glowed sometimes.

And I slipped, the broom having lost the wet battle underfoot. Oz caught me, but the hash plopped on the floor.

I stared at the little pile of pink mush. "It accessorizes the rust and water just right."

Oz barked out in laughter, and I was seized in a fit of my own. I didn't know what the hell was so funny, but I couldn't stop. In my attempts to regain control of myself, I slipped again. I seriously needed a real crutch.

Oz stabilized me. "Careful there. I only have enough wrap for one more ankle. I can't wrap your whole body."

I laughed again. Oz and I, trapped at Magic Powers Motel, in the worst conditions imaginable with hardly any heat, laughing as we stood toe-deep in ice water with brain eating amoebas.

This was ludicrous.

But I wouldn't trade it for anything. My laughter suddenly died down.

Oz followed suit. "Can't say I've ever laughed so hard at hash before."

"Let's hope the rest of it is just as energizing," I said. "That was better than a jolt of caffeine."

"I think we should find out," Oz said, offering me another bite.

As we locked gazes, I kept breaking out in small chuckles, picturing another plop on the floor. But I kept myself together long enough to close my lips over the spoon. Oh. My. Damn.

It was amazing. I swallowed and groaned. "That's seriously the best thing I've tasted...all day."

"You have a very low bar." Oz set the spoon down with a grin and lifted the spatula. He moved the sizzling food around.

Perhaps it wasn't so low anymore, and now it was my turn to confess. "I never did something like that before, you know, show myself to a human."

Oz paused, the spatula frozen in the air. He slowly turned toward me, his handsome features a mix I couldn't quite place. "I had a feeling."

That wasn't enough. "What I'm trying to say is my running away wasn't entirely your fault."

Oz set the spatula down and gave me his full attention. "Then what really kept you away for five years?"

I had been afraid and ashamed, and I couldn't face him, but he knew that, so I said simply, "Dignity."

"That's a pretty good excuse."

"I thought so." Every aching move I made reminded me of the accident that left me stranded here. I couldn't hate that deer anymore.

"You know what I think?" Oz asked, leaning close. So close I could smell those sexy notes of his. Those sexy...human...notes.

"What?" I asked, breathlessly.

"I think you should kiss me."

II
Picnic

Oz

THE OLD DARBY I'D loved all this time was still in there, and I somehow managed to drag her back out. With one difficult-to-pry, understandable explanation, Darby and I were back right where we'd left off. Right inside this very motel, just after she'd shown her deer to me. Except this time, she was still here. I only wished our time apart hadn't been wasted, but I was happier now than I was in the last five years combined. One kiss would be a new beginning.

It wouldn't be enough. I could never get enough of her, but I was a patient man.

"Kiss me," I repeated, prowling closer until I could breathe in her unmistakable scent. Darby Hanson, sleek deer, gorgeous human—both inside and out. I knew the inside quite well, but her shifting for me had been but a tease. I wanted more. I wanted to carry her over to a bed and make her scream my name until she forgot hers.

Darby's gaze shifted to the spitting and sizzling stove. With a trembling voice, Darby said, "The...the uh, food's burning. We should eat."

The rejection stung, but not as much as her vanishing on me five years ago. Before asking, I'd braced myself against Darby's fickleness. She wanted me. That much was clear. I just couldn't figure out her hesitation, and I happened to love a mystery. "What kind of rescuer would I be if I let my patient starve to death?"

She chuckled.

I turned off the burners and began filling the plates.

"Where are we going to eat? There aren't any tables. The bar doesn't have any stools."

This wasn't a problem. We had the couch that folded open into a queen-sized bed—although lumpy and unstable. We also had the armchair. Darby making it a problem meant she wanted to be close to me. I'd happily oblige.

"Picnic by the fireplace it is. I'll meet you over there."

Darby's sly eyes shifted over to me. "Is this a date?"

She was teasing me, but I liked this playfulness. I wanted to see where it went, so I sent her mock horror. "I would never be that crafty."

Darby laughed and hobbled out of the kitchen on that terrifying broomstick. And yes, I paused to watch her sexy ass. Then I did a breath check, which seemed fine to me. With a shrug, I gathered up the dishes and balanced them carefully as I brought them out to the crackling fire. Darby had settled on the floor. I wished I had a blanket for us to sit on or curl up with. And pillows. Clean, fluffy, soft pillows.

I handed her a plate and lowered the rest to the floor. I sat next to her.

"This is nice," she said, spooning up a bite of hash. "Not quite the blood of my enemies, but considering the circumstances, I can't complain."

"I'll take that as a compliment." I tested an expired peach slice. It wasn't half-bad, and so far, didn't cause me to run to the restroom.

"You should," Darby said. "I fully understand I'd be dead if you hadn't found me. I would've been trapped in my car and engulfed in flames when the engine blew. Eventually, I would've been buried under a thick blanket of snow, and who knows how long I would've been there, waiting for someone to notice I was missing and to find me. Maybe I would've been unconscious when I died—I can only hope. So, if it's not clear, thank you for saving my life."

If I hadn't been around, she wouldn't have crashed in the first place. I gave her a tight smile through my chewing.

"Weird though," she added. "I remember something strange."

My stomach swirled, and I had to blame it on the peaches. I reinspected the next forkful for mold, but it was clean. "What's that?"

"The car door was missing. When you lifted me out, I didn't bump against it, and you didn't duck around it. When a car hits a tree, the door doesn't just...fall off."

Er, no. No, it didn't. I swallowed. "I'm sure your memory is just spotty. You took a good knock to the head. How's it feeling, by the way?"

"Better." Darby smiled and scooped up more hash. "Being stuck here reminds me of how this village is one giant missed opportunity."

I was feeling plenty of missed opportunity lately. I wanted her to continue, to wish the same thing I wished. "How so?"

"Small towns don't offer much. Oz, you saved my life. You kept us alive and mostly comfortable in a blizzard, and you fixed the front door. Oscar Martin has so much more to offer the world than handyman skills. You should've been so much more."

She was calling me a loser for not having a career like my brothers. Awesome. That felt...great. "I have the freedom to create my own schedule, and people around here need me, even if they can't afford much. I like repurposing and upcycling. I also happen to enjoy *fixing* things." I gave Darby a meaningful look, but I didn't think she caught the message.

"This entire motel needs to be fixed," Darby said absently.

I'd noticed. There was something about this old building. It was simple, easy to fix, and it held a lot of memories for us both. I could picture it all fixed up, warm and cozy again. "And it's got great land, lots of old forest, and it's peaceful out here."

Darby slurped up a peach. "If the documents didn't specify family had to take it, I'd give this old place to you. It's perfect for you."

She was right, but there was no point in daydreaming about it. As she'd said, this motel came with strings, and I wasn't at the end of any of them. Hopefully, whoever she picked to take over would fix it up just the way it had been. Then we could celebrate like old times. "Our families are doing the combined festivities again this year."

Darby flicked her gaze around the motel and frowned. "Where?"

"Same place for the last four years. You should come."

Waiting for her response was like a slowly twisting knife. She'd wanted my kiss but wouldn't take it. Now I was offering her a real date, something she'd choose and not be forced into. A bolder move, but I couldn't imagine standing before our families again without her by my side.

"If we get out of here on time, I'd like that."

My stomach fluttered. "We will." I'd make sure of it, even if I had to burn the world down to get us there—I gazed out the bay window—or shovel until my heart exploded.

12
Perfect

Darby

THIS RIGHT HERE—A PICNIC by the fireplace—reminded me of old times again, but there was one key difference. Oz used to shoot longing gazes across the room, and when we were alone, he'd shower me with thoughtful gestures. Oz had been beautiful and shy. Sweet and kind, and he'd been trapped in this village. For whatever reason, his parents favored his brothers, and that wasn't fair. Oz deserved better. He deserved better than all this, and I admired his ability to make lemonade out of lemons. He'd also blossomed in other ways, too. For example, his incredibly healthy and strong physique. He definitely got the best of the Martin genetics. And he was a survivor with a heart of gold, no longer shy, but still respectful. All this change—him learning who he was, finding happiness, and growing into assertiveness—all happened while I was gone.

Oscar Martin, a human I had no business with, had been happier and better off without me. We could enjoy this snowed-in vacation, as much as we could, while worrying about the propane level in the tank, and then I needed to leave. I had Shauna likely worried about me, or at least dying with curiosity, and I had a boss who expected me to punch in for my shift tomorrow. I wasn't sure how that was going to happen yet. I really wished I could give Oz this motel. It was like the two of them were meant to be. But instead, I had to hide my true self from my family for yet another holiday gathering. Then slink through the crowd, begging someone to take over this dump. And hope I didn't get fired in the end.

I swallowed another juicy bite of peaches. I'd already polished off the hash, and after our laughing fit over the plop landing on the wet kitchen floor, I didn't think I could look at hash the same way again. The food was pretty damned good, but Oz had always been a great cook. Great at saving people, fixing things, surviving in a blizzard with bleak conditions. He was...perfect.

"What's wrong, Darby?" Oz set aside his finished plate. He'd left exactly half of the food for me, even though he'd need more than I did.

What I needed more was an excuse for my sudden derailing thoughts. "My ankle still hurts."

Oz shifted his weight and beckoned for my ankle. I swung it over. He rested it in his lap and inspected the wrap. "It's loose. I'll rewrap it. Hold tight for me, because this might sting."

Oz's sensuous touch, the brushing of his fingertips, the firm grasp—gentle but caring—made me close my eyes. As he rewrapped my ankle snugly again, the pain I'd been ignoring eased.

"Is that better?" he asked.

I wanted to say it was perfect, but that wouldn't exactly be true. "As good as it's going to get."

Oz didn't move my foot away. "Listen, we need to have a quick chat. I hate to spring this on you, but I need you to be as prepared as possible."

Those words always preceded really bad news. My dark thought spiral captured my throat and threatened to drag me back down to a place where I couldn't breathe, couldn't function, and stewed over regrets. We were holed up in a dump, so the only thing Oz wanted to let me down easily with was him leaving. But he couldn't leave me now. Not like this. I put on a brittle but strong face. "Let me have it."

"There's enough dry cordwood to get us through another night, but the propane tank will be empty before then."

He...he wasn't leaving? Relief relaxed every muscle in my body until the gravity of his solemn warning sunk in. Without propane... "No more cooking, toilet, or heat in the building?"

"Just this fire until the wood's gone. I'd winterize the toilet and sink since we used them, but there's no anti-freeze. I already checked."

"When we thaw out again, fire hoses everywhere."

"Basically," Oz confirmed.

I sighed. At this point, I should probably bulldoze the damned place and sell the empty land.

"You don't care about this place enough for that to bother you. What else is on your mind, Darby?"

I had to tell him the truth. Better now than after expectations were framed and hopes were built. Forming the words was harder than I imagined. I had to practice them in my head, brace myself for the change in his features, and suck in a breath. "Oz, I'm not staying."

He grinned. "Oh, but you are. Neither of us is getting out of here until Rusty frees us."

Why was this so hard? "That's not what I meant."

Oz's lightness faded. The disappointment and ache on his face was hard to see. "How long until you disappear again?" he asked a little coolly.

"Right after the Christmas holiday party."

"A few days?" he asked. That painful coldness lingered, and I didn't blame him.

"I have to get back to work. I didn't request time off. This was a lucky break in my schedule."

Oz set my foot aside and added a few more pieces of cordwood onto the pile. "Unless you have a snowblower, we're still stuck together. Your boss is going to have to get over it."

I shifted my weight on my aching hip, and something caught my ear. "What's that?"

"What's what?" Oz asked, suddenly on alert, eyes drifting toward the kitchen.

With my sharp senses, I picked up something faint, but it was there. I focused, putting all my effort into teasing out that one thread of sound, and there it was. I grasped it and followed it as it grew.

"Do you hear that?" I whispered and staggered up to my feet and grabbed the broom.

Oz straightened and listened, and I swore he paled. "The plow."

"It's here." I grinned. "We're out of here."

I carefully got to my feet while Oz rushed through the kitchen, made metallic and wooden thumping noises, and came rushing back with a shovel. I raised my brows while he struggled to open the front door. The drift that greeted him somehow didn't deter him. Oz shoveled fiercely, like his life depended on it.

Well, it sort of did.

Quickly, he made a narrow path and ran out, waving the shovel in the air and shouting. Rusty wasn't going to hear Oz over the noise of the metal plow scraping against the highway, but perhaps he'd notice the orange flag of a shovel. Oz would do anything to make sure we got to that Christmas party.

Or maybe he was tired of my gloomy company.

Or maybe he didn't want to freeze or starve to death.

I wasn't entirely sure which of those possibilities motivated him, but either way, he was wildly full of energy.

The grinding noises slowed, and shortly thereafter, Oz returned, coated in a fresh spray of snow. He shook off inside the doorway and rushed toward me with the excitement only a rescue could bring.

"We're getting out of here." He lifted me in his arms and spun me in place. When he slid me back down to my feet, he kissed me—a quick press of his lips on mine.

My stupid heart fluttered.

Oz snapped back, as if realizing his mistake. "Oh, I'm sorry."

He was right to be sorry. He shouldn't have done that. All it did was complicate things that had no business being complicated. But I wanted Oz so badly. I wanted to tear off his clothes and take him right on that lumpy old mattress. I wanted to explore places I hadn't seen. After all, he'd seen me naked. It would only be fair. I was tired of holding back, and since he'd already crossed that line, I threw it away. "Don't be."

Oz searched my eyes, hesitating for only a moment, and this time, he kissed me slowly. The kind of kiss that wasn't impatient or nervous. It wasn't the kind testing the waters or learning. It was a confident, sensuous kiss, and he leaned into me, urging me for more, trying to take all of me right here. It was the carefully crafted kiss all those years needed answering—all consuming, completely blinding, fully distracting, and...

...more amazing than I could've ever imagined.

The plow's bellowing horn honked, pulling us apart. I gazed into Oz's eyes, and a rush of heat tore up my cheeks. I couldn't keep the smile off my face.

"Rusty freed us." Oz gave me a crooked smile and touched my chin to draw my eyes. "Stay here."

"Thank you, Captain Obvious." This time, it was playful, and not at all condescending.

Oz rushed to the door, and to flag down Rusty, he waved. I glanced at the lumpy mattress with longing. Was I right to skip the chance to have sex with him?

Before I could picture the lost opportunity, Oz strode to the fireplace and pointed at the armchair. "Grab your purse. We're going."

I hobbled a few steps and slung my purse over my shoulder, double checked my phone was still there and not dead. Hopefully it lasted, because my charger was in my car. After hastily putting out the fire, Oz returned to my side. I expected him to support me with his shoulders. Instead, he scooped me up into his arms. I let out a surprised yelp, and Oz swung me through the door and closed it behind us.

"Is Rusty giving us a ride?"

"He can't."

"Ambulance?" Not that I needed a medical bill to drown me.

"Not exactly."

"Then what?"

Oz didn't answer. He marched across the uneven, snowy parking lot and headed onto the road. Rusty honked and waved through the driver's window and rumbled down the snow-covered highway.

"Are you really going to carry me all the way to your Jeep?" I asked with amused disbelief.

"You have strong legs, but mine are better."

He was a human, and as much as I adored his heart being in the right place, I was heavy. I was a burden. "Oz—"

"Arguing won't change my mind." Oz marched along without missing a beat or panting, as if I weighed nothing. Today, he was my hero.

13
Picky

Darby

HE STILL WASN'T TIRED by the time we reached Riggs's bar. Oz had settled me gently onto the uneven snow covering the parking lot, and he brushed off his Jeep. He tried to carry me into the vehicle, but I protested and climbed up myself. When we'd missed the turn for my parents' house, I was surprised. And when he turned down the road for the urgent care clinic, I was a little relieved.

"You don't trust your handiwork?" I teased.

"My brother is better than I am. You need someone qualified to look at that, and I don't want you to suffer long-term problems because I couldn't get you here on time."

"My injury isn't your fault."

Oz gave me a thoughtful look and pulled up to the drop-off door. "Give my regards to Jasper."

"You're not coming inside?" My disappointment was difficult to hide.

"I have a few things to take care of," Oz said flatly.

Right. He'd been trapped with me. Life didn't stop because we weren't participating temporarily. "Be safe."

I climbed out, closed the door, and waved as Oz drove off. Watching the taillights glow brightly as he stopped to turn, I had to wonder if whatever that magical moment we shared was nothing but a fantasy of two people with nothing better to do. The real world swooped back in and sent us back on our way. I wasn't sure I liked that at all.

Darby

Oz's taller, older brother could've been his twin otherwise, but my heart didn't flutter when Dr. Jasper Martin's penlight flashed in my eyes. Still nothing special when his gloved hands manipulated my unwrapped ankle.

Jasper whistled at the damage and looked over his shoulder at the lit x-ray images on the screen. "Quite the doozy you got here."

"Car accident," I said.

Jasper's brows lifted. "Oh? How did you get here?"

"Oz."

Jasper nodded with a smile. "He's got the nose for tracking damsels in distress."

I frowned. I wasn't a damsel, but, yeah, I had been in distress. I let it slide. "He does."

"Where is my baby bro? He didn't tag along?"

"No."

"Huh," he said dismissively. "Not surprised."

I didn't know if that meant anything or not, but since I was stuck here for a while, curiosity got the better of me. "What does that mean?"

Jasper tucked his penlight into the breast pocket of his lab coat. "Darby, my brother never went on a date the entire time you were gone. Many have tried—flirting, buying him drinks, stuffing their numbers in his pockets—but he only left disappointment in his wake."

I couldn't imagine why. Five years was a long time to be alone. Then again, I hadn't dated anyone, either. "Sounds like he wasn't interested."

"I'm sure the right one is out there. Harvey and I have tried setting him up, too, but he's stubborn."

I smiled. "He sure is."

Jasper turned my ankle. "He's looking for something that doesn't exist."

"What do you mean by that?"

"Our family is picky," he said simply.

"The Martins never minded my family," I said, trying to pry more details. My family successfully kept their wolf side a secret from the humans, so I really didn't know what Jasper referenced.

Jasper pressed his lips thinly. "Appearances can be deceiving."

I frowned. "Are you saying your family *pretends* to like mine? They've been celebrating Christmas together since we were kids. You know, that annual party that's this weekend. Are you going to be there again?"

"Of course," Jasper said stiffly. "Your mom wouldn't let us live it down if we skipped. Are you going to be there?"

"I will be."

Jasper's warmth faded. Oz had been right. His older brother still had an ego problem that years of treating Aunt May's gout pain and Uncle Frank's hammer-smashed thumb hadn't cured. I never did like Jasper all that much, and like Oz, I had a life that kept moving and things to do. "What's my prognosis, doc? Am I dying?"

"It's sprained, not broken. Keep it wrapped, minimize your boot use, take anti-inflammatories around the clock, and keep it raised as much as possible. You'll be fine soon."

And with my shifter side, rapid healing should be complete in a few more days. "Great. Time for me to go."

"I'll get your paperwork together."

With discharge paperwork in hand, I sat in the lobby. A decorative bough of pine rested on the registration desk with blinking lights and fake poinsettia. A miniature Christmas tree sat in the corner of the room with paper decorations made by the staff. I couldn't get into the festivities this year. My mind reeled with everything that happened, and I realized Oz hadn't come back, which I'd stupidly hoped for.

I pulled my cell phone free and actually had an okay signal in here. Shauna had texted me, eager for an update. I replied that everything was fine. I confirmed the motel was a mess, and the plan hadn't changed. She instantly badgered me with questions about my ex. I shouldn't have told her about Oz. He wasn't my ex. I didn't know what he was.

When Shauna was satisfied, I needed to get out of here. Oz hadn't returned, so I wouldn't ask him. He'd done more than enough for me lately. More than I deserved. Shauna was too far away. My friends moved on without me when I'd vanished on them. That left my parents.

With extreme hesitation, I called my parents for the first time in a long while. I'd been sending them Christmas cards and politely declining their annual party invitation, but we hadn't talked much beyond that. I hadn't explained to them my humiliation, and I certainly didn't want to talk about the fact that I wasn't like them.

Surprisingly, Dad was excited to hear from me, even more so that I was in town, but when I explained where I was, Dad insisted on rushing to come get me. A round face with salt-and-pepper hair and a Santa-style beard grinned broadly at me. Toss in a red plaid shirt over jeans with suspenders, and no one would mistake him for anyone but Dennis Hanson.

My dad loved football, beer, and deer hunting season—what wolf shifter wouldn't? After years of begging, I'd finally agreed to join him at his blind when I was seventeen years old. I didn't have any interest in hunting, but I wanted to spend time with my dad, and I felt guilty for rejecting him so many times. The whole while we sat in the blind, silently watching for an unsuspecting deer to stumble our way, my stomach churned. I couldn't handle the idea of my dad shooting someone like me, if any others existed, and I couldn't imagine the look of disappointment and shame when he found out. I hadn't managed to tell him, and when I held the rifle to my shoulder, aiming at a buck, I wanted to vomit. My hands trembled.

I'd squeezed my eyes shut and fired.

The buck jerked to the side and leaped out of sight. Dad and I tracked blood for a while, but with no snow to guide our path, and fading daylight, no deer had ever been found. Dad was disappointed we didn't have meat, or a pair of antlers to display on the basement wall, but he was proud I took the first step in hunting like a real Hanson. He'd tried to comfort me by explaining vomiting after the first kill was normal.

That didn't help. After we got home and I showered, washing myself over and over, I never hunted again. Dad claimed he didn't mind. Shooting animals wasn't for everyone, but there was an undertone of expectation there. Wolves had a duty to hunt and catch prey to feed the pack. It was our nature.

But not mine.

"Hey, kiddo. Welcome back." Dad hugged me, squeezing the crutch between my arm and my ribs. It hurt. He pulled back and inspected the inflated boot on my ankle and the overpriced crutch under my arm. "What happened?"

I preferred Oz's support. I'd settle for the broom. I didn't want the bill for this fancy thing, but after Jasper's weird story, I accepted it just to get away from him. "Simple math, Dad—blizzard, plus deer, plus tree."

"Those damned deer. Such stupid animals. Where do you think 'deer in the headlights' came from? They see something right in front of them, and they stand there. Just stupid. Tasty, though."

I glanced at the floor and tried not to shiver. "Yep," I quietly agreed.

"Let's get you home." Dad meant his and Mom's house, not my apartment. No matter how much time had passed since I'd moved out, they still considered my home to be theirs. It was sweet, but a little annoying. Considering my options, I rolled with it. The big party was in a couple days. I needed to call in sick to work, and I needed a slam-dunk presentation to ignite the starry dreams of one of my cousins. Someone had to want that ticking time bomb of a motel. Yeah, that one with the flooded kitchen.

"Where's your car?" Dad asked as he drove the plowed roads.

"Crumpled against a tree on highway 41."

"I'll get Harvey over there to tow it to his shop. It'll probably take weeks to get the parts in and fix it right. In the meantime, you can have your old bed."

"I have to work, Dad. I can't stay."

Dad's expression was flabbergasted. "But you just got here. Tell me you're staying for the annual party. The Martins will be there."

"I'll stay for Christmas." I could figure out a good enough excuse for a few extra days off. I hoped.

"Great! We're having an ugly sweatshirt day. Where's your luggage?"

"In the car."

"You can wear my sweater from last year. Your mother's been making me a new one, and she's confident I'm going to win."

I sighed...silently. And rolled my eyes...secretly.

Welcome home, Darby Hanson.

14
Let Go

Oz

I HATED TO LEAVE Darby alone at the clinic with my brother. I could imagine all the crap Jasper was telling her—more like subtly warning her about. Darby didn't know, like hers, my family wasn't human. I'd promised I wouldn't tell Darby's family what she shifted into, and it was the easiest promise I'd ever made, because I hadn't and wouldn't tell mine, either.

But just because we were all part of the hidden world, didn't mean we all got along. My family tried to treat the Hansons warmly, but the truth was we were enemies, predators of a different kind...except me. The annual Christmas party had always been tense. But a little alcohol—not too much to make a disaster out of everything—helped loosen the Martins from their constant defensiveness around the Hanson wolves.

When Darby had left, I'd been equal parts devastated and relieved. And now that she'd returned, I beat back equal parts of excitement and an intense need to protect her from the second hidden layer right under her nose. Darby was better off not noticing the undercurrent of tension and danger here. I couldn't be selfish. Her crash, her being stranded here, was strictly my fault, so I had to do what I could to make it right. Because as much as I hated to admit, I alone couldn't keep her safe from the Martins.

I called my older brother Harvey and explained the situation. Harvey was a great mechanic, and his repair shop was the best in town. That wasn't much of a metric, considering his was the only repair shop in town. But he maintained a scrap yard behind the shop, and I swore he could get anything we needed. I trusted his opinion. Harvey drove us out to the accident scene, and when he spotted the snow-covered tin can thoroughly kissing a tree, he lifted his hat and scratched his head.

"The driver survived?"

"Darby."

"Oh, that explains it. Well, these old cars crumple easily to cushion the driver, but this... Nothing short of sawing off the entire front end and welding on a new one is going to work."

"It's totaled?" I figured as much, but it was hard to hear.

Harvey chuckled. "What part of that do you think is fixable? The frame is bashed in. The structural integrity is compromised. It's not road-safe anymore, even if I could fix it."

"Everything can be fixed with time and the right tools," I insisted.

Harvey chuckled. "And you're going to heal this car with a magic touch, is that it?"

I frowned.

"Well, it can't stay here." Harvey hooked up the cable to the rear axle and slowly freed the car from the tree with a few snapping and crunching sounds. He dragged it up through the snow and onto the flatbed. When the remains of Darby's car were fully secured, Harvey climbed back into the cab and brushed snow off himself, letting in a gust of winter's wind. He rubbed his hands together and blew on them for warmth. Harvey should've been able to handle the cold better than me, but I wouldn't raise suspicion by teasing him.

Oh, but I wanted to.

We gazed at the mangled car—Harvey with fascination, and me with dread.

"Not everything can be fixed, Oz. Sometimes, you just have to let go."

I couldn't, and I wouldn't, but that was a 'me' problem.

Harvey pulled out onto the highway, yellow warning lights flashing. "I know you don't want to give up on it, but listen, the airbag didn't even deploy. I'm guessing she couldn't afford the repairs on it lately, so she probably wasn't doing maintenance, either. She's lucky to be alive, but wolf shifters are a tough bunch. Maybe she'll be happy to pick out something new."

"Right," I said, dismissively. I didn't want her to pick out something new. I wanted her to have what was hers. I wanted to make her whole again, as if I hadn't ruined her life. But if I couldn't get her car fixed, then I had to figure out something else. "Drop me off at the hardware store on your way, hey?"

"Sure, whatever."

Darby

THE HOUSE WHERE I grew up smelled exactly the same as I last remembered, instantly pulling me back to the day I left. I dropped onto the couch as the TV droned on about an upcoming Christmas-day football game. I didn't pay it any attention. Humans throwing around balls made of animal skin made my...well, skin...crawl. Dad was in charge of setting up the outside display and making sure all the lights and inflatables worked properly.

Mom was baking whatever would stay fresh until the party, as usual.

And every year, my job was to decorate the inside, but the house already looked like the North Pole had invaded, except there wasn't a tree yet.

"Need any help?" I asked Mom.

"I got it, dear," Mom said, whisking a mixture in a bowl.

Deer? I did a double take at her word. "What?"

"I've been doing this myself for five years now. I can handle it." Mom poured batter into paper cups lining a muffin pan.

I got it. Mom was upset I'd jumped ship five years ago and hadn't returned to help out or celebrate since. They didn't know I left because I couldn't handle hiding myself from them anymore. I'd shown Oz, and his reaction was nothing short of a nightmare. And he wasn't family. He didn't have...expectations.

Come to think of it, for a human, Oz did handle it remarkably well, not that I had other experiences to compare to. And I shouldn't have been so upset with him or afraid of whatever repercussions awaited, causing me to leave in the first place. If nothing else, I could trust Oz.

But my family's shock would be far more dramatic. Far more disastrous. Far more consequential. I only needed to survive a few more days. I shot a text to my boss, making an excuse for severe sickness, but the message only swirled. Internet access was like a leprechaun up here. Catch it if you can, otherwise the prize was gone. I sighed and tucked my phone away.

Dad approached and lowered himself in the squeaky recliner across from me. "Hey, kiddo. I called Rusty for a tow, but he said your car isn't there anymore. Someone else must've got it. My bet is on the Martins. Harvey's always looking for an easy buck."

"Dad, Oz was with me. He probably asked his brother for the tow." Entirely unnecessary, but the gesture was both noted and appreciated.

My defense of the Martins went by without a comment, and for the first time, I picked up Dad's undercurrent of ire. I tried to think of other situations to explain Dad's intolerance of the humans, but I couldn't picture any. I wondered what the reason was, but I didn't want to talk to him about Oz.

"I called your insurance to get a claim started, too, but you don't have full coverage." Dad's judgment now shifted to me.

I couldn't afford it. In shame, I shook my head and looked at the carpet. Worn, old, but clean. Nothing ever changed.

"Well, that's unfortunate," Dad said. "Guess you'll have to buy a new one."

"I'll figure it out." Another time. I sent him a reassuring smile, but Dad assessed me with that critical eye of his. The one that also made my skin crawl.

"Alright, kiddo," Dad said, finally relenting.

I had to get out of here. "Can I borrow the truck?"

"Of course. Just don't crash it." Dad pointed to the key rack by the door.

I was never going to live that down. With weighty embarrassment and shame, I flew to the key like a deer chased by a wolf, ignoring my inflatable boot's groaning and my ankle's annoyance. In another day or two, I'd be fully healed, anyway.

Capturing the key fob, I jumped into the truck and headed across the village. The snow-plowed-but-still-messy roads to the hardware store gave me flashbacks, and even in broad daylight, I kept watch for deer. I slowed into the parking lot, but the snow was more slippery than expected, and I slid a little too far for comfort. Thankfully, Dad's newer truck remained unharmed. I exhaled a breath of relief.

I pushed through the door, ringing the little bell, and I rubbed my arms against the cold and widened my eyes. Holiday decor had been splashed all over the store. Lights strung around the register blinked cheerfully, manned by one of my cousins, and pine boughs were strapped around the door and hung along the ceiling. It was pleasantly festive.

I headed straight to the automotive department, which was two aisles near the back of the store, but the shelf labeled with the anti-freeze tag was empty. I ducked low, looking for those perhaps misplaced jugs, but I couldn't find them, and I couldn't leave without a solution to the impending disaster.

I headed straight for my younger cousin, who was snapping gum in his mouth and scrolling on his phone. I wanted to ask if he had internet access in here, but I was too frustrated to bother...and a delightful opportunity popped into my head.

"Hi, Aaron."

My cousin looked up. "Darby? Long time no see. What brings you here?"

"Anti-freeze. The shelf seems empty. Do you have any left?"

"Sold out."

"What?" I asked, exasperated. Aaron's uncomfortable expression had me chill out. He didn't need to know the extent of the motel's problems. "Okay. When's the next truck coming?"

"With the holidays, tomorrow's delivery will be delayed until next week."

Next week? That was it then. In the next few hours, we were floating just above freezing temperatures, and since Oz and I used the sink and toilet, the moment those pipes froze again, *hisssss*. Or whatever sound uncontrollable, high-pressured water made while spraying in a small room. I took a few deep breaths. "I'll figure something else out, thanks. But I have a question for you."

Aaron blinked, not anywhere remotely as cheerful as the decor between us. I supposed that meant I could ask freely.

"Do you like your cousin's liquor store?"

He made a dismissive snort. "You mean the products? Sure. Who doesn't like a drink? Riggs's place is too expensive these days."

"I mean, would you want the opportunity to run a business? Quit here and have the independence and freedom of ownership?"

Aaron lifted a brow. "Are you offering?"

"I am." I smiled, simply giddy with anticipation. "I have a motel that needs new ownership. And it's free, if you're worried about that. I need to find someone who wants to take over. How does it sound to be self-employed? Be your own boss, run the show, and make the rules—and your schedule? Doesn't that sound like a great opportunity?"

Worded like that, it kind of did, but Aaron's interest evaporated. "I'm not touching Nana's motel. Nope. Couldn't even pay me."

I still had hope. "It's just like we remember. Sure, it needs a good cleaning, but it could be great with a few repairs and some fresh decorations."

Aaron lowered his phone. "Darby, you haven't been around for a while. I don't think you understand the condition it's in."

Ha, ha, I thought sarcastically to myself.

"It's not worth fixing," he added. "Even if it was, the business isn't here anymore. Do you see the customers around you?"

To humor him, I looked around. We were the only ones in the building.

"Powers is dying. That motel isn't worth reviving, even if it was in great shape. And face it, Magic Powers Motel should be demo'ed. Is there anything else I can get for you?"

"No, you've done enough."

Aaron lifted his phone and returned his attention to the screen. I walked back to Dad's truck, empty-handed and discouraged. I thought I'd sold it well. I was almost convinced myself, but maybe Aaron was right. The repairs were overwhelming, and the business wasn't here anymore.

But Oz had fixed the kitchen sink—one repair of how many? I could watch Oz fix anything. All. Day. Long. I smiled to myself and headed back out.

15
The Setup

Darby

I AWOKE IN MY old childhood bed. Same bedding. Same curtains. Same furniture. Even my pictures, now curled with age, were still tacked to my corkboard. I skimmed over them, my eyes settling on a group shot of me as a cheerleader with the squad. I'd been smiling awkwardly and shyly next to the other girls—humans. But that difference wasn't the source of my discomfort.

At that age, impending shifter puberty made me very self-conscious. My mom was tasked with *that* talk, and she'd only slanted it toward the inevitable shift into a wolf. Unlike the werewolves and other weres, who were controlled by the power of the full moon, shifters could change into their animal at will, and during shifter puberty, it could happen by accident.

That talk had been the night before this photo, and it was firmly on my mind while trying to smile. Every moment until my puberty finally happened, I'd been terrified I'd break bones and grow fur like a Chia pet on fast forward. And then the screams...

That was a miserable time for me, but wasn't high school for everyone? Looking back on it now, I hated every minute of being a cheerleader. I dug deep to figure out why I'd joined in the first place. During those years, I had been a loner, for the most part, a believer in quality over quantity. And I didn't have enough in common with most others to truly connect. My parents encouraged me to get out of the house and make more friends, but that wasn't why.

I'd been alone. Okay, that was a factor, but one I'd been living with, so I couldn't blame loneliness on a psychotic decision to join the cheerleading squad, of all things.

What else had it been? Then it came to me. In standard stupid teenage fashion, I'd overheard Oz talking to the boys on the football team. Oz preferred shop class over football. But when a pair of linebackers explained to him only cheerleaders were the right caliber dating material, he'd agreed. I had to join.

I placed a palm over my open mouth. The photo next to the school-spirit-fueled group shot was Oz and I smiling with our heads touching. We'd been to one of the earlier annual Christmas parties, when the motel had been in its heyday. Now I truly saw what I'd been missing.

I hobbled on the boot out to the living room as fast as I could, almost certain I could shuck the thing for good today. But Dad appeared expectantly, fully clothed for the outdoors.

"Something wrong with the Santa display, Dad?"

"Something's wrong with the living room."

Puzzled, I tilted my head and glanced around. In the kitchen next to us, Mom wore a festive apron, hair teased and sprayed to new heights. She slammed the oven door closed with her hip while balancing a tray of cut-out sugar cookies. That was completely normal.

Decorations had filled the small house. Everything smelled like fresh-baked cookies or freshly cut pine. The standard scent of Christmas. "I don't know, Dad. What's wrong?"

"We need a tree, kiddo. It ain't Christmas without a decorated hunk of Mother Nature in the living room. Come on, get dressed."

Mom huffed at Dad's crass description.

"I'm a bit busy, Dad." I had important things to do, and I had to see Oz.

"Too busy for a tradition you abandoned?"

Put like that, I couldn't turn down father-daughter bonding time. "Sure, but we're going to have to take your truck."

Dad laughed. "And I'm driving. Apparently, you need more lessons on how to avoid those dumbass deer in snowy conditions."

I looked at the carpet and grumbled about making it to the store and back just fine. I knew he meant well, but the way he said it hurt. That was my fault for not explaining why, but I couldn't bring myself to do that either.

"Let's go. We need to get the thing decorated before your mother has a hernia."

"I heard that," Mom called over, annoyed. I didn't blame her.

Dad drove us to the Christmas tree farm, where we had to cut down our tree of choice fresh from the land. I struggled with this. I always had, but maybe I could convince Dad otherwise now that I'd returned. Maybe since I'd returned, he'd be more lenient in listening.

"Can we get an artificial tree this year?"

Dad made a dismissive noise. "Plastic? You want a *plastic* tree. You'd rather give your money to a store selling plastic Chinese trees shipped across the ocean, polluting the water and the air. How does that sound better than a locally purchased live tree, which is replanted every year?"

During his charged rant, I couldn't get a word in. I didn't realize Dad was so passionate about the topic.

"Think about this," he continued. "If the Parkers couldn't sell their trees, because you and everyone like you chose Chinese trees, what do you think the Parkers would do with this land?"

I gazed out at the bright, snowy acres with similar sized spruces and firs in neat rows and tidily sheared to make the desired conical shape. Since Aaron had said the town was declining, I didn't picture much, if anything, would happen to it. "I don't know."

"If they couldn't sustain themselves selling and *replanting* their trees, then they'd have to relinquish it to a developer. And you know a developer would lowball them because of the location. Not many people like to live up here, away from the crowds and whatever security they get from their concrete forests. Now this cold corporation needs to recover its costs and earn a profit—because that's what companies are. It's what they do, so this assumption isn't an assumption at all. This is exactly what would happen. Our big, evil company would cut down *all* the trees for processing. It could leave an endless field of stumps, destroying our environment entirely. Or if they believed they could lure enough humans, they'd build something that takes away from Mother Nature. I mean, I love a casino as much as the next guy, but you can't frolic through it chasing rabbits. And more humans means more traffic—more chances for us to get hurt, killed, or even worse—discovered by those humans. Thankfully, Michigan was smart enough to keep wolves off the hunting list, and that's why I'm never leaving the state. And now that you're home, you're safe, too." Dad shot me a warm smile.

To me, this wasn't home, but Dad careened way off topic, and I'd rather argue about trees than me staying in Powers. I'd known Phil Parker in high school, and he seemed nice enough. I didn't want his family's livelihood destroyed, but I couldn't agree with Dad. "But you're killing a tree and throwing it away weeks later." Watching the trees shrivel and die on the curbs just killed me. At least the city mulched them for landscaping. But that didn't ease the sight of them all lined up for shredding, like fallen soldiers awaiting a violent burial.

"You won't convince this old coot to switch to plastic trees. And now that we're here at the Parker's tree farm, I have someone you need to meet."

I didn't like surprises. "Who? And why?"

Dad grinned with a spark in his eye as he climbed down out of the cab. I had to walk in deep snow to pick out a tree for my dad to murder, so I slipped off the inflatable boot, flexed my ankle, and slipped on a thick-lined winter boot. I tested my weight on it before standing fully and climbing down. It didn't feel weak.

Dad approached a worker on the farm and shook hands with him, beaming proudly in a way I hadn't seen before, and my heart sunk down into that boot to be squashed. I approached slowly, taking care of my ankle, because I didn't want to visit cryptic Dr. Jasper Martin again. When I reached Dad, he was standing with a man about my age with a scruffy beard and wearing a plaid coat, a floppy knit hat, and black steel-toed boots. Add in suspenders and toss in a couple of decades, and they could've been brothers. I bet this new friend of Dad's loved hunting, football, and beer, too.

Dad hugged my shoulders, and I finally recognized those eyes. We might've had classes together, but we didn't know each other.

"Darby, this is Phil. Phil, my daughter." Dad re-introduced me to my old classmate, Phillip Parker, son of the farm's owner.

He carried a short chainsaw in his leather-gloved hands, and when he offered me the empty one, I shook it. "Nice to see you again, Darby. It's been a while."

"It has," I said politely and dismissively. Didn't take a genius to figure out what Dad's intent was, but I had no interest.

"Phil's going to be at our dinner tomorrow," Dad said proudly.

I faced Dad with utter disbelief. "But I thought that was a Hanson-Martin tradition?"

Dad leaned in close. "So was your attendance." That...wasn't fair. "Your mother wanted me to introduce you to John's boy. The Parkers are members of the nearby wolf clan."

Wolves were territorial, and I was surprised the Hansons coexisted with the Parkers all this while. "I didn't know," I said to Phil.

"Me, neither. Cool though, huh?"

Ignoring that, I asked either of them, "Can we cut down the tree now?"

Phil offered me the chainsaw. I supposed I could appreciate him assuming I could use one. That was a nice change of pace.

But Dad intercepted it, and Phil looked at Dad apologetically. "Take your pick of the trees. When you're ready, I can help load it into the truck."

"Thanks, Phil," I said and grabbed Dad's arm to drag him away. At his size, no one could make Dennis Hanson do anything, but he moved his feet with me. This ridiculous setup was my family's attempt to get me to stay, and the audacity angered me. If I didn't need a family member to drop a rotten motel onto, I'd skip this dinner party entirely.

But then I wouldn't see Oz.

Dad glared at me as we headed for the coniferous rows. "That wasn't nice."

"Setting me up without advanced notice isn't *nice*."

"If you had a warning, you wouldn't be here."

"Then what does that tell you about how this would go?"

"We only want to see you happy, kiddo."

Dad and I strolled the rows of thick trees, his attention on the selection, while I glared at him, careful of how far my voice carried. "And pushing a stranger on me would do it? If he wasn't a shifter, would you still approve?" The words tumbled out, at first as an insult about Phil, but then I had to know the answer...for Oz.

Dad stopped and faced me. His tone was a warning. "Darby."

I'd already been lectured today. Now it was his turn. "Just because someone isn't here on my arm doesn't mean I'm available. And I want to know, Dad, would it matter if he were human, seriously? Or am I required to find someone like us? Because, in case you haven't noticed, there aren't that many of us around here."

"You know the risks of exposure."

He wasn't talking about the freezing temperatures, and I was well aware of the rule. "I know, Dad."

"It's not safe. You have to trust me on this. We keep track of each other. We protect each other. Us wolves have to stick together." Dad hugged my shoulders again. "That's why we're helping you."

Well, that was loud and clear. Oz, longstanding family friend, wouldn't be accepted into the Hanson household.

"Dad, I'm not interested in Phil."

"I wish you were."

"I'm happy the way I am. Isn't that enough?" My question wasn't about Phil. It really wasn't about Oz, either.

"We don't believe you are happy, Darby."

I couldn't change what I was, so I didn't know what to think of that.

Dad continued his hunt. "We have to search high and low, narrow down the choices, and pick the perfect one. We can't disappoint your mother."

I thought that was too much effort for a tree.

"Keep your eyes peeled," Dad added. "We gotta get the best one."

They all looked too similar to me, with variations in height and width. Some were fuller and some thinner. This search seemed pointless. "What do you mean by 'the best', Dad? We have our own measure of what we want in a tree, and none of them are better or worse. One just fits right, regardless of what others think."

Dad stopped. "That's what I mean. Find the one that fits right."

The images of me having joined the squad for Oz, and the photograph of Oz and I smiling for the camera returned to memory. But I wasn't flushing with excitement.

Dad cheered at a fluffy seven-foot spruce. "Look at this, kiddo. When you stop looking too close, sometimes the right one is right in front of you. What do you think?"

I didn't look at it. "What if Mom doesn't approve of the right one?"

"Are you kidding me? Look at this thing." Dad fired up Phil's chainsaw, and I plugged my ears.

I wished I could have a real conversation, but Dad wouldn't listen. He couldn't see what I yearned to hear. Instead, my wolf shifter family, a wolf visiting in our private territory, a deer shifter they'd rather eat, and a family of oblivious humans were joining together under one roof. What could go wrong? Well, this was going to be the worst annual Christmas party ever. I bet myself fifty bucks on it.

And I was going to win.

16

The Answer

Oz

AT RIGGS'S BAR, A television blared in the corner with some Christmas movie on repeat. I didn't know, couldn't focus. Sort of the point of coming here. I stared at my empty glass, debating another. I was a lightweight, but tonight, I'd earned it.

"Another whiskey sour?" Riggs asked.

"Neat, please."

Wintry winds hadn't let up today, but thankfully the snow did. Sun had shone on Rusty's plow job, making the white roadway slick with patches of ice. The usual winter in northern Michigan.

Riggs mixed the drink. "Tell me, what are you doing in my bar on Christmas Eve? Don't you have any last-minute shopping to do?"

Feeling called out, I glanced over both shoulders. No one remained but me and Riggs. "I could say the same for you."

The middle-aged bartender, passionate about his life's work, grinned. "The missus does all the shopping. I'd rather be here. Catch the few stragglers who need a little pick-me-up." Within moments, he set a stout glass in front of me. "Lemon?"

I waved the offer away and downed the glass in a rush.

Riggs collected the empty and set about mixing another. "So, what's eating at you?"

As a second-generation bar owner, Riggs had heard everything imaginable, and at the moment, there was no one here to give unwanted opinions, so what the hell? "I'm in love with a woman."

"I can see how that's a problem." Riggs slid the next whiskey sour my way and leaned against the bar, analyzing me. "But just to be clear, what *is* the problem?"

I snorted. "She's leaving the day after tomorrow. Made it clear from the beginning, and I did what I could to help her leave sooner." I drank down that one, too, the warmth heating my stomach, but the alcohol was too slow to numb my skull.

"You love this woman?" Riggs repeated, a solution working through his mind.

"Yep."

"Does she know it?"

The kiss had been fairly obvious, and I figured by now she would've caught on. But perhaps not? "I never told her."

Riggs snorted in self-satisfaction. "Tell her, dumbass. Let her stew on that information, and she can decide for herself what she wants to do with it."

I had to put my heart on my sleeve for her, face devastating rejection, humiliation... What the hell? I had to do for her what she'd done for me. That was the answer all along.

"But if you don't do anything, you'll be here every night, lining my pockets, wondering what could've been. Choice is yours."

I rose, and a knowing smile lifted Riggs's lips. The bartender rubbed the bar surface dry.

"You know what? Thanks, Riggs. I'm going shopping after all." I dropped a wad of cash on the bar, which Riggs promptly pocketed, and I rushed out the door.

That man might spend all day pouring drinks, but he was a genius under all that beer.

Oz

WHEN RIGGS SHOWED ME exactly what I needed to do to win over Darby's heart, I'd rushed off to get it, but that small unorthodox trinket wasn't enough. I needed to do more. I needed to show her how I felt and make things right. My brother's grim diagnosis meant I had to replace Darby's car, and thankfully, Harvey had a few to choose from. It wasn't exactly the same make and model or year or color, but objectively, it was better. And she deserved better. Right after the purchase, I was ready to declare my undying love for her, but I had to figure out how to present these two things. Turned out, I had no gift wrap, and on Christmas Eve, no less, I'd beat the clock to the store.

Darby's cousin had been manning the register. He'd said if I returned for more, I was out of luck. The store was sold out until next week. I figured as much, since I bought it all, but that wasn't what I'd come for. I'd told the young man I was in desperate need of gift wrap. The kid lifted a brow, clearly having never been in an emergency Christmas crisis before, and sold me a shiny roll.

I needed half the damned roll to make a presentable wrapped gift for Darby. It was a lot harder than it looked. I hoped she didn't laugh at it, but I was willing to take the humiliation and embarrassment—for her. And this wouldn't even be comparable to what she'd done for me, but it was a start.

My brother paid an employee to deliver Darby's new car tonight, and on Darby's doorstep with the key in my pocket and unorthodox gift in my hand, I lifted my fist to knock. Since the motel had been removed as the venue, the Hansons hosted the Martin-Hanson annual Christmas party in their cozy home, and to make up for the lost swagger of the motel's heyday, Mrs. Hanson fixed a feast. But this year was different.

I held the unorthodox gift in my hand, the shiny bow glinting the light from Mr. Hanson's abundant decorations. So very different.

Nerves skittered along my stomach, and then the deep rumble of an approaching truck had me smiling. Delivery as expected. I waited until Harvey's guy finished lowering the car to the snowy roadside and gave me the thumbs-up.

Then I finally swallowed back my nerves and knocked.

Darby answered with both surprise and stilted awkwardness. Her beautiful cheeks reddened. She wore a hideous sweaterdress belted at her waist. It hung to her mid-thighs, which were covered with festive red leggings. Something about the ugly design was familiar.

"You look perfectly hideous," I said with a grin.

Darby blushed and pulled at the bottom hem as if showing off her outfit. "Think I'll win?"

"Isn't that your dad's sweater?" I knew I recognized it. He wore it last year, and he didn't win.

The blush returned, and Darby cracked a soft smile. "Happy Holidays. Want some eggnog, or do you want to go straight to the hard stuff? I'm feeling the need for copious amounts of alcohol."

Like me, Darby wasn't a drinker, but I understood the need to disappear at family events. Having been away for five years, she might be rusty.

"I'd rather talk."

"Sure. Come, uh, come inside." She scanned the street, and her eyes moved right past her new car. She was nervous, but I gladly entered, and then I stopped short, seeing the reason for her hesitation. Someone I recognized sat on the couch, fingers between his knees and nervously fidgeting. I stepped up to her shoulder and whispered with dread, "Why is Phil Parker here?"

Before she answered, I ferreted out the explanation for the son of the tree farm owner, who was a member of a neighboring *wolf* pack, visiting conveniently the same year Darby returned. My dread needed company. Welcome, existential dread. At certain low points in a man's life, wondering if the body could register pain on impact with a train had been an experiment I'd considered conducting. Although I'd never stepped in front of a full-speed train, I was completely certain what my heart just did felt exactly the same.

Chest squeezing, gut punching, knee-buckling, crush of any and all hope.

"My dad invited him," she whispered.

I'd been cast right back into the friend category in Darby's life, and this pip-squeak was supposed to take the place I wanted, but I wasn't giving up that easily. I'd waited for Darby for years. Phil Parker? Hardly a speed bump. I gave Phil the evil eye, but he didn't pay any attention to me.

"This is for you," I whispered back.

"You didn't have to."

"I did," I insisted.

"Thank you." Darby grinned and tucked a lock of dark curled hair behind her ear before accepting it. I wanted her to open it here, but as custom, she set her gift under the tree with the others. Watching her sexy ass bending in front of me, a fresh whiff of spruce reached my nose. I gave Phil the side-eye again. I guessed Mr. Hanson just picked up the tree at Phil's farm.

Toddlers ran around, squealing and drooling. Their mothers, my cousins, chased them. My older brothers were already here, and both shot me gazes expressing the discomfort around the strange wolf in the house. Despite Phil's appearance, there was no awkwardness for me. I gave them a silent wave, and reassured, they returned their attention to the laughter in the room. Everyone was obliviously happy for the holidays, as usual, except for me and Darby. I didn't think Phil was too excited, either. Good.

Dad was on the other end of the couch, watching the football game with Mr. Hanson.

"Oscar Martin, we've been expecting you," Mr. Hanson said loudly.

I approached him in his recliner and shook hands. The big fella didn't stand, but I didn't fault him for it. "Does this mean I'll be allowed in the kitchen this year?"

With a beaming grin, Mr. Hanson said, "Not a chance. If Lucy sees you in there, she'll toss you straight out. You know how she gets."

I chuckled, and the old man returned his attention to the game.

"Oz," Darby said, gripping my arm as a buoy in this tension-filled ocean of drama. "What did you want to talk about?"

I tossed a look at Phil and said, "Not here."

"Then let's go." She pulled my arm, and I wouldn't resist her for anything. Darby brought us outside to her front porch, and

I hoped she wasn't kicking me out. But I wouldn't leave until I gave her the key. I dug into my pocket. "Just you and me, Oz. What's up?"

"Why do you want to talk out here? It's freezing," I said, worried about her discomfort in the sweaterdress.

As if that was the cue, Darby folded her arms together for warmth. I took off my coat and rested it over her shoulders.

"The motel had space. Room to escape. This house...is suffocating," Darby said.

This was her childhood home. She loved it. I believed the suffocation to be entirely the presence of the unwanted wolf shifter. Now I could fix that problem. I freed the key from my pocket. "Then this will cheer you up."

Darby looked at it, puzzled. "What's this for? Did you find the key to Nana's quarters?"

I pointed at the curb a few vehicles down along the sidewalk. "That red car over there is yours."

Darby frowned. "What? What do you mean 'mine'?"

"I ruined your car. I'm sure you heard Harvey can't fix it, so I replaced it."

"Oz." Darby dragged out my name and held the key back at me, but she wasn't looking at me. She gazed with desire at the car. "I can't accept this. It's too much."

I didn't take the key back.

Darby faced me, and I gazed into those big brown eyes I fell for so long ago. I opened my mouth to say the words I needed to say when the front door opened, interrupting me. Phil popped his head out. "Uh, Mrs. Hanson needs the gravy stirred."

Darby frowned. "I never make the gravy."

"I can do it," I said. "Want to watch me try?" I gave her a saucy grin, trying to remind her of our time at the motel together, cooking inedible canned goods and surviving alone. Keeping warm, alone.

Darby relaxed and chuckled, and to Phil's dismay, I followed on her heels. Darby returned my coat and headed over to the couch. I hung it on the coatrack with everyone else's and slid into the kitchen smoothly, suavely. Mr. Hanson gave me a warning look, but he didn't know Mrs. Hanson's game with me.

"I'm reporting for gravy duty, Mrs. H."

Mrs. Hanson raised her brows at me and winked. She raised her voice. "Get out of my kitchen. This is a woman's place!"

I bit back my grin. The patriarchs—and likely my brothers—snickered and joked from the living room. No one laughed when they ate the food, though.

"Think they bought it?" she asked playfully.

I lifted the corner of my lips. "Always do."

And I was always teased about it, but I didn't care.

17

Too Late

Oz

POTS BUBBLED AND BURBLED on the stove. The running oven warmed the kitchen comfortably, and the scents of ham, potatoes, and pumpkin pie filled the space. Peanut butter, chocolate chip, gingerbread, and iced sugar cookies with a holiday motif lined trays off to the side. It was chaotic, yet peaceful. Reminded me of our house at Christmas, too, but there was nothing like this annual tradition. The only thing that had been missing finally returned.

A timer went off, and a pot boiled over, sizzling the flame.

"Can you grab the cookies?" Mrs. Hanson asked while turning down the temperature and dashing for a towel.

I stuffed my hand into a mitt and freed the cookie sheet from the oven. They looked delicious and almost machine perfect. "Want me to ice these when they cool?"

"Nah. I have a batch ready for icing. I can handle making deer antlers." She smiled to herself. "That's my favorite part."

"What is?"

"The irony of eating deer cookies." She looked at me with shock and worry. "I mean, Rudolph is adorable."

I snorted. "He sure is."

"While I ice these, can you get the gravy?" Mrs. Hanson asked.

"My specialty."

I shucked the mitts and stirred the gravy. Most heathens would eat it as is, but I turned the burner down and stirred, but not too much to break the starch.

"I'm glad you're here to help. Darby's terrible in the kitchen."

I figured 'terrible' meant not up to Mrs. Hanson's standards, and I didn't appreciate her criticism of her own daughter. Darby was great at many things, but I was glad for the chance to talk about her. "What's up with Phil out there? Is he a visiting relative?"

"Him? Oh, no. Phil is a special man Dennis found for Darby."

Despite the heat in the kitchen and my accurate assumption, my blood chilled. "Is that so? How does she like him?"

"Not sure yet. But they're a great match."

Continuing this conversation was physically painful, but I had to know. "Why do you say that?"

"They're both the same...kind of person." She hesitated in explaining. Darby's parents still didn't know she wasn't a wolf shifter—like little old Phil out there, and I'd promised not to spill the beans.

"Is that so? They both love eighties hair bands, eggs with ketchup, and Pilates? I didn't pin him as the type."

Mrs. Hanson eyed me with either suspicion or frustration. "Not like that. They both want the same things."

"Like what?" I pressed.

"You know, a family, a nice house. Things everyone wants," Mrs. Hanson said generically, trying to avoid explaining to me.

I hadn't been aware Darby wanted kids, but her mother's description was oddly vague...a safe *assumption*. "Darby never mentioned a nice house to me."

"Women don't tell their best friends everything, especially those like you," Mrs. Hanson said, avoiding my gaze.

And there was the crux. These wolf shifters had to know about us Martins—and recently, because that was the only explanation for Mrs. Hanson's sudden disapproval of me after all these years. And that was also a reasonable explanation for the Hansons suddenly setting Darby up with another wolf shifter. They didn't approve of me. Offense curled under my skin.

"Is the gravy okay in here?" Darby popped her head into the kitchen.

That was my call to swoop in for the rescue. I cleaned my hands with a towel. "Gravy's thick and smooth, Mrs. H. If you need anything else, give me a holler."

With Mrs. Hanson's slight scowl, our game had ended. The Hansons used to like me, but she thought I was a threat to Darby's future. Why didn't my family tell me the Hansons knew about us? That would've been big news.

But I doubted they *really* knew about me, since my own family didn't.

I allowed Darby to coax me out of the kitchen. "Save me from this, please," Darby whispered and dragged me to the living room.

"My pleasure."

I would save her from anything...even her own family.

Darby

TO AVOID PHIL PARKER, I'd worked the room, playing the gracious host, and I'd struck up conversations with every cousin I had. Those with kids distracted them from my pitch, and those without, had boredom glazing their eyes. A few outright told me they appreciated the offer but 'no way'. Maybe I should've crafted up some charts with numbers or something. Most concerning, everyone agreed the motel used to be the pinnacle of Powers, Michigan, but that day had been long over.

Oz might've given me a generous gift, allowing me to go home, but not one of my cousins would take the motel off my hands, leaving me still trapped here. On the topic of that gift, Oz and I needed a real conversation. I thought that kiss had been in celebration of our freedom from entrapment. And I believed I'd wrongly indulged in his touch a little too much. I shouldn't have done that, because I was leaving soon, and I thought Oz understood, because he'd been cool after I told him I was heading back to Green Bay, Wisconsin. But then he'd carried me all the way to his Jeep. I could've hobbled or hopped or used the broom. He'd insisted, confusing me, but he'd dropped me off at the clinic with short and cold sentences, leaving me to believe he truly understood, even if he didn't like it.

Then he bought me a car. Of course, I couldn't accept it on principle, but I couldn't just stuff the key back into his coat. He deserved a better explanation than finding such an extravagant gift rejected like that. When Harvey arrived at the party, he'd warned me my crashed car wasn't repairable. No amount of magic could straighten the frame and make it structurally sound again.

I was crushed, lost, disappointed, and once again angry at the dumbass deer.

Except that deer brought me that lovely escape with Oz for the short while it had lasted, and Oz brought me the red sedan. It was beautiful, sleek, and so much fancier than my beat-down...uh, beater. But why had Oz insisted my wreck had been his fault? That guilt made no sense. Oz did seem more empathetic and kinder than most human men, which was why he'd been my best friend, my crush, for *years*.

He and I needed to clear the air between us, and I needed an escape, somewhere quiet and private. I couldn't breathe in this house. This was just like all the previous annual Christmas parties—except there was nowhere to hide. To decompress. I wished Oz and I were at the motel right now.

I wished *only* Oz and I were at the motel.

Instead, Mom shoved this stranger on me, and Dad kept encouraging it. I felt bad for Phil, having been tossed to the wolves...ha. I wasn't sure if he caught my avoidance, or if he held onto hope of something between us, but it wasn't going to happen. And Phil's last friendly wave sent me over the edge. I wish

I could've pulled him aside and cut him free before anything embarrassing happened. But we didn't get a chance. I wasn't brave enough to explain to everyone why our visitor left before the food was served.

So I did the only thing I could think of. I found Oz and dragged him from his favorite place—the kitchen. "You don't mind leaving your bat cave, do you?"

Oz chuckled. "Not at all. I'm surprised your mom didn't throw me out of there the second I stepped inside."

"You know she secretly likes your help." And hopefully that the rest of the Martins and Hansons teased him behind his back for it. But I thought there was nothing sexier than a man who knew his way around the kitchen. A man who knew I loved eggs and ketchup and knew how to prepare them.

Oz smiled.

"Can we take a minute? I'd like to have a chat with you somewhere less...gossipy." And out of sight of my blind date, who had less chance than a snowball in hell. Or my car against a tree. The weight of the red car's key suddenly felt so much heavier.

"Sure. Absolutely." Oz scanned the bustling house for a temporary sanctuary.

But it was too late.

18
Defense

Darby

MOM CALLED FOR DINNER to be served, and everyone rose at once, like starving wolves to a fresh kill. I cringed at the eagerness, and I dreaded not having time alone with Oz, and I dreaded even more that my dad seated me next to Phil. Oz sat across from me. While freezing outside and wearing Oz's coat, I hadn't noticed his perfectly ugly Christmas sweater. It was blindingly bright green with Santa bent under a tree. The focal point was nothing less than Santa's huge, red ass. I cackled, and everyone turned to me.

My face burned bright. "Um, Oz's sweater is awesome."

The Hansons and Martins—I didn't look at Phil because I didn't care—scrutinized Oz's outfit against their own, but Oz looked only at me. He'd removed his hat, and his thick, blond hair was still smashed on his head, but the little curls remained around his ears. Those thin but angular lips quirked up. He and I were against this chaos. He and I with a shared secret—my secret—hidden from all the others. I smiled back.

After our families, and probably Phil, determined Santa's ass wasn't more interesting than the food, bowls and plates were passed around. Metal scraped at plates, spoons scooped at pasta dishes, and cookies were lifted off a tray and handed over.

A few of my family members chuckled at the cookie design, and when the plate reached me, I saw why. My stomach clenched at the deer cookies. My family eagerly vacuumed them. Bunch of animals.

"Rudolph, Mom?" As in, not me? I didn't have antlers or a red nose, but I needed some reassurance.

"Of course, dear."

My spine stiffened. Was all this a joke? Did they know and were mocking me?

Oz, of course, gave me a crooked smile in empathetic solidarity.

"Phil," Dad said. "You hunt? Of course, you do. A tree farmer, outdoorsy guy like you, has to hunt."

"Uh, yeah," Phil said nervously. "I like it as much as the next guy." Poor Phil didn't know what to say, surrounded by a neighboring wolf shifter pack, a bunch of humans, and...me.

"Well, ain't that a coincidence? Darby hunts, too!"

The Martins only looked at me with conversational interest while politely eating. But my family was fascinated, even my distracted cousins with toddlers making dust out of cookies in their laps.

"It was one time, Dad. I didn't like it, remember?"

"You should've seen it," Dad said to Phil, ignoring me and using his hands—and spoon—to recreate the scene. "We watched the idiot thing walk right up to us. Didn't catch our scent. We were downwind, you know. And the meaty buck strolled right on up to our bait, as if asking to be dinner. It was a harsh winter that year. A single blast to the chest was an easier exit than starving. So hey, we were going to grant its wish."

I looked at Oz, wanting to scream at my dad to shut up, but Oz studied me, pulling me from that anxiety and growing panic. He sent me empathy...or guilt? Something was there on his handsome face. Oz wasn't a hunter. I didn't know if he understood how hard it was to kill an innocent animal—one that looked exactly like me. My only solace—I later found out after we'd searched—was my target survived.

"Darby, she had the buck in her sights. All lined up perfectly. She held her breath, and with a little excited encouragement on my part, she squeezed one off. The damned thing was so close it was impossible to miss, but Darby nailed the hip instead of the lungs or heart. Beginner's nerves, right, kiddo?"

Oz still watched me.

Without letting me answer, Dad continued, "You know, or maybe you don't, the best kill is the instant drop. Don't want the things to suffer, right?"

A few murmurs of agreement on both sides. Phil smiled, enthralled with my dad's embarrassing tale of yet another way I'd disappointed my family.

"The damned deer bolted off into the woods, startled by the crack of the rifle. *Bang!*"

Dad imitated my shooting the gun with his spoon. "I chambered the next round, hoping it would've collapsed nearby. Even back then I was too old to follow blood trails for hours. And we didn't have snow yet that year, so the trail was harder to sniff out. Dear little Darby couldn't stomach tracking her dinner's body. I think Bambi scarred the girls."

A few snickers from the Hanson men had me squeezing my fork. Oz still watched me, features darkening.

"So," Dad finished to a captive crowd, "we never found it. Poor thing probably starved to death. Maybe something else ate it because it was wounded. We'll never know."

At least he didn't mention how much I vomited after. Dad had *some* tact at the dinner table.

"Oh, that sucks," Phil said confidently after hearing my dad's stance on the question. "I'm actually a great shot. Never lost a deer yet." Phil gave me a look like he was trying to impress me. "I can take you hunting, Darby. I can help you find the fun in it."

I gave Phil a blank stare, completely shocked by the offer. While my dad set up this ridiculous blind date, did he not once mention

I hated hunting? I wanted to decline, but I didn't want to embarrass my dad in his own house, and even if that weren't a factor, Phil didn't give me a chance to answer.

"No offense, sir, but I bet she'd like it after I take her," Phil added proudly.

"That's a great idea!" Dad bellowed, laughing alongside his perceived perfect match.

That didn't just happen, did it? Wide eyed, I glanced around. My mom grinned with approval, but the Martins only watched with keen and polite interest. They weren't nearly as entertained by my failure to kill a deer. Or Phil's offer to teach me the right way. Or whatever possible hidden message Phil may have been suggesting. This wolf shifter wasn't taking me anywhere.

Phil grinned, self-satisfied, and he forked up a bite of ham.

"Sure, she's not good at murdering animals," Oz said, interrupting the rambunctious Hansons...and Phil. They quieted down with his words. "Because Darby's compassionate. She'd rather destroy her own car—her only way home—than harm an animal incidentally on the road. To me, Darby missing her target could be explained by one of two things."

"And what's that?" My dad asked, entertained but slightly annoyed by his story being scrutinized.

"She didn't *want* to kill an innocent animal, so she missed the shot on purpose."

A few Hanson wide eyes turned on me, as if that was the greatest shame the family had ever heard.

"Darby wouldn't do that," Dad said, dismissively. "The hunt is for survival, Oz. We're not slaughtering defenseless animals in a pen like meat-eating humans do. Hunting is a fair game of survival."

If the wolf shifters got too upset, I was afraid a growl might escape. The Martins weren't safe here.

"It's not survival anymore," Oz countered, surprisingly quite passionate about this old story. "We're civilized. Have been for a long time. The other explanation for Darby missing her shot was she'd been uncomfortable, nervous...*pressured*, so she missed on accident."

I exhaled. Both Oz's possibilities for my missing the shot were direct insults to my dad's character—revealing my defiance to his awful orders and questioning Dad's parenting.

Either way, Oz insinuated my failure was Dad's fault, and I agreed.

Mr. Martin hushed Oz, and they argued in a whisper for a few seconds. Mrs. Martin played with her spoon, staring wide-eyed at her plate. This was a disaster, as I'd expected, but it could always be worse. I just wanted my dad to stop talking so we could eat in peace and leave. But Dad didn't like being questioned, insulted, and embarrassed in his own house, which was why I declined to say anything, but the words couldn't be shoved back down, tucked away, burned. Tension hung like suffocating curtains.

My cousin's toddler made a combination of spittle and a chuckling noise, and he leaned forward and slapped the sweets tray, stealing another deer sugar cookie. Into that gooey maw of his, another deer died. I swallowed a dry lump in my throat and grabbed my water.

It didn't help.

19

The Reveal

Darby

DAD WASN'T AMUSED BY Oz's assumption. "Of course, she was pressured," Dad said, exasperated. "As a teenager, Darby was a chicken, and she needed a shove out of the nest to grow up and become a real Hanson."

Chickens didn't nest in trees, but that was beside the point.

Plate half-finished and completely ignored, Oz's gaze never left me, and his warmth returned. "I wouldn't force her to do anything she doesn't want to, and even if she wanted to impress you with her hunting skills, she didn't need to. Darby is great at other things. Things that matter much more than her aim."

I wished I knew what was going through his head, but I certainly appreciated him defending me. As usual, the Hanson men wouldn't give me five seconds to collect my thoughts and argue. Even if they did, everything I said would've been dismissed. But I believed Oz would've listened, and he would've defended me, just as he was now.

I wished I hadn't been so boneheaded to have missed what was right in front of me all those years ago. I wished I had more of a spine to face Oz's reaction to my rule-breaking revelation. I wished a lot of things happened differently, but I couldn't change the past.

"Like what? It's not driving!" Dad barked out fresh laughter.

"I can drive stick, if you need lessons," Phil whispered, leaning close.

"No, thanks," I whispered back.

"The fact that you're asking me says more about you," Oz said, chin held high, and I could feel my face burning bright.

Dad got quiet really fast. "Excuse me?"

"I'll give you a few ideas for next time," Oz said. "You know, a reference, so the story doesn't bleed with disrespect. Darby's great at thinking on her feet in emergency situations—within a split second, she *chose* to crash her car instead of hit the deer. She's not a terrible driver. I'd say she was excellent at navigating treacherous weather."

I smiled. I couldn't help it.

"And she's got a perfect aim. She chose to hit the deer's hip, a non-fatal, hardly painful, location on a deer's body, rather than kill it or make it suffer."

I hadn't thought of that before. I didn't want to kill the deer with Dad's rifle, but I didn't want to disappoint Dad either, so I went with door number three—exactly what Oz assumed. I'd shot the deer, but I saved it from death or suffering.

"And despite that, she's pretty decent in the kitchen, too."

Dad scoffed and pegged Oz with a glare. More silent discomfort around the dinner table.

"You weren't there either time, so your nonsense is only that—an opinion formed from some fantasy," Dad said with a tone of condescension. "Maybe Lucy would like another hand in the kitchen?" Dad erupted in laughter at his own question, and a few snickers from the Hanson men grew into more laughter. And now, after a dinner's worth of awkward silence, the Martins joined in. Most of the suffocating, overstuffed house was laughing at Oz. My best friend, my rescuer, sat taking it. His face was familiar, one I knew so well—the face that tolerated family's crap, because that was what family did.

I could handle my family teasing me because I knew nothing different. And when I found out I didn't get the wolf gene, I had to grow thicker skin and learn to hide my true feelings...my true nature. But to insult Oz, who'd always been there for me, was my limit. I abruptly stood, knocking my chair to the floor with a startling clatter.

Martins and Hansons quieted expectantly.

Not knowing what else to say to redirect them away from Oz, I said, "I'm getting rid of the motel."

Dad's laughter died instantly.

Look at that, I'd finally managed to kill something.

Oz paled.

"What did you say?" Dad asked accusingly. "Please, come again, because these old ears thought they heard something impossible."

Oz said to him, "She means there's mold, a serious case of mold, but we'll take care of it."

Oz faced me with a silent message to stop or rethink this decision. I'd always planned to rid myself of the motel—the only thing tethering me to my family. And after tonight, I couldn't look at them.

I added, firmly and clearly, "The law firm, on behalf of Nana, explained I can run the motel or hand it off to family. And as many of you have already heard tonight, I choose to give it away." I addressed everyone loudly. "Now's your last chance. Is there any Hanson who wants a free motel?"

Whispers and murmurs settled behind my words. "It's got a great location, spacious rooms, a commercial kitchen, and living quarters above the lobby. The fireplace is huge and welcoming, and there's a perfect spot for a giant Christmas tree. Travelers come up just for the location, you know that, and it's popular for cross country skiing. You've all been there. We used to celebrate there. Who here wants to bring that memory back?"

Damn, I almost sold it to myself. Except for its current condition... The future exploding pipes and toilet—thanks to my cousin's lack of anti-freeze... And my current anger at my family. It wouldn't be the first time nostalgia bit me hard in the ass, but this time, it was too late to change my mind.

"Is that the Magic Powers Motel you're talking about?" Phil asked. "That place is a dump."

Family around me mumbled, and Dad rose, face burning bright red. But his anger wasn't directed at Phil Parker, who said the quiet part out loud. Nope, Dad glared right at me. I could take it. With Oz safe from my dad's fury and scrutiny, I could take anything.

"You want to *give away* Nana and Gramps's legacy? Why? For what? To run back to the city? What's out there that we can't give you?"

Support. Kindness. Understanding. Respect. Things I didn't realize I didn't have. Not really. I mean, I knew how they'd react. I knew what they'd say, so I spent a lot of time quietly stewing to myself. I looked at Oz. I think I always knew, but tonight Oz shined a spotlight on my family. He was my rescuer again. With him at my side, I could've stood up to them back then. And now that Oz was literally on my side, and I was standing...

I wouldn't back down.

"Like Phil said, the motel is a dump," I said evenly. "It would need a year to fix it up and deeper pockets than I have. It's not a gift of a family legacy. Dad, it's a burden. Nana dumped it on me—*little Darby, let her deal with the mess, the family screw up*." I mocked a voice that didn't exist. Perhaps it was the one festering in the back of my mind. At least, I left out the evil cackling. I thought I got my point across without going too far.

Dad flinched, as if he'd never considered how his hurtful words made me feel. "Why would you say that?"

"Oz was right." I looked at my best friend, who was now blinking back tears. I hoped his family hadn't hurt him that much. But they were probably just as awful to him as mine were to me. Even as humans, we still had much in common. "I couldn't shoot that deer, Dad. I tried to fake it so you wouldn't be *too* disappointed. And I chose to hit the tree, so I didn't kill another deer. I'm not like you, Dad. I'm not like any of you." I couldn't change the past, but I could change the future.

The Martins were human, and exposing myself to those outside of the hidden world was forbidden. But I'd done it once, and nothing bad happened—other than the total destruction of my self-esteem and lost time with Oz. Phil was a wolf, as was my family. I was tired of being treated like I was less than, and this time, I could face the reactions.

Of all of them.

"Darby?" Oz asked gently. He was worried about what I was going to do. He was right to be worried.

"I warned you," I said to Dad. With a challenging scowl, I headed for the door, ripping off Dad's hideous Christmas sweater and kicking off my painful heels as I moved. I threw open the door and darted into the snow, but I didn't feel the cold.

Under the glow of the front porch lights, and bathed in Dad's Christmas lights, I spun in my underwear and red leggings to face my family and Oz's. Meeting the gazes of everyone crowding the porch curiously and some bashfully, I shifted.

I *shifted.*

My leggings and underwear tore under the strain of my animal form. But I didn't care. I wasn't afraid of their reactions, but most importantly, I wasn't afraid of Oz's this time. I needed him to see. Oz pushed his way through to the front of our families, mouth gaped like the others.

With my head held high, I absorbed the gasps, the shock, the whispers. Shouts for those remaining behind, to wrangle the toddlers, echoed across the snowy village on a darkened Christmas evening.

That's right, people. I'm a deer.

20

The Catalyst

Oz

SHE DID IT. DARBY had the strength to do what I never could. She was inspiring, and I couldn't have been prouder of her than at that moment until I heard a growl. Then I'd never been more terrified.

A wolf's growl.

My family wasn't threatening her—they weren't wolves. And a Hanson could fight the hunting instinct to protect their own family. I turned to find the threat moving aside, eyes dilated, peeling off his clothes. This was worse than a nightmare. Phil Parker—unwanted guest—was shifting into his wolf form. His aggressive, lowered stance and bared teeth threatened Darby's life.

Darby's elongated ears repositioned, tracking the threat. She had amazing control over her deer instincts. She must've been terrified, but giving in to the fear would result in a hungry chase. I pushed through the crowd to pacify the unwanted visitor.

As I moved, my family tore off their clothes, preparing to shift in response. I thought they had more control than that, but a feral wolf was a threat to my family, too. I wanted to hope my family was protecting Darby, but I wasn't sure they weren't only defending themselves.

Gasps came from Darby's family, and there was an answer. Mrs. Hanson did not know we were shifters, too, and I basked in the delight of shocking the bloodline purist as I pushed through, heading for Phil.

A whole clowder of bobcats, who would also, no doubt, love a tasty bite of venison, formed an offensive stance. I slipped around them, tripping once on their piles of clothes and shoes, and I reached Phil's side. But in response to the rapidly escalating threat, Darby's family shifted into their wolf forms.

Me shifting would be the final straw to begin the bloodshed, and because I would save Darby from anything...even her own family, I remained human. I spun, at a loss for how to slow this disaster. Somehow, I had to remove the catalyst without triggering an attack or chase. Rather than try to reason with everyone's feral animal sides itching with the urge to maul, I ran into the house and grabbed a blanket off the couch. Rushing back outside, I pushed past the snarling animals and darted up to Darby's deer. I threw the blanket over her tan, fur-coated back and draped it around her muscular shoulders. Her ears twitched toward me, but she didn't leap away.

"Darby, shift back now, or they'll attack."

The wolves and bobcats, with swiping and squabbling among them, stalked toward us, climbed down the stairs, or leaped off the porch and into the snowbanks. Snarls and snaps had me swallowing a lump in my throat.

I moved in front of Darby, facing them. "Stop! All of you stop. What are you thinking? This is Darby. You can't attack her. She's family!"

They didn't stop advancing. Darby should've waited until after dinner to do this. At least they wouldn't have been as hungry.

I had to convince Darby to shift—to speak to me, and the easiest way was to confess something that needed answering.

"Darby, listen to me. This, all of this, is my fault." Her big doe eyes blinked at me, and her ears twitched. She was listening, but she needed more. "Your accident was my fault. I know you don't believe me, but it was...my...fault. You hear me? If I hadn't been there, none of this—" I waved to the advancing animals, "None of this would've happened. I'm sorry."

Our families trudged through the snow, an easier task from my broad-footed bobcat family than the wolves. Both families navigated around Mr. Hanson's extravagant holiday display. One bobcat, I thought Uncle Mike, leaped up onto the highest snowbank. Low growls permeated the winter night air. Clouds of breath puffed and dissolved under the porch light. Everyone was lit from behind by twinkling Christmas lights, which put a new spin on the nightmare before Christmas.

"Darby, please."

Darby shifted back into her human form and held the blanket tight over her naked body. I exhaled in relief. The wolves and bobcats stopped advancing, their prey having disappeared. They looked around, confused, and the humans within regained their control. Most of them, Phil included, retreated into the house to find cover and shift back.

Darby faced me with tears in her eyes, and all I wanted to do was scoop her up into my arms and whisk her away to safety. I wanted to comfort her—hold her until the tears retreated. I wanted to kiss away her pain, and I wanted to use my mouth, my body, to make her forget everything that ever hurt her, and I wanted her to feel pleasure she'd never felt before.

I wanted to make her happy.

Darby

My leggings and undergarments rested in tatters on the snow. I trembled under the blanket, standing naked and barefoot in the snow during Christmas in Michigan. Clouds of my breath were carried away by the soft breeze.

In embarrassment and shame of my deer shifter side, I'd bolted for the city when Oz hadn't reacted as I'd hoped. I assumed it was because he was horrified I wasn't human—which was certainly a logical thought process. But now I knew it was because his family were predators, and I was their natural prey. Oz had been terrified his family would hurt me. He had been afraid of hurting me.

Oz was a bobcat shifter. All this time—years of school classes together, sharing family events together, being best friends—and he'd never told me. Keeping his secret after I'd shown him what I was hurt worse now than it did then.

And his confession, knowing what I was, broke my heart. He caused my accident because he'd been chasing the deer I swerved to miss. My ankle was sprained because of him. I'd had a concussion because of him. My car had been totaled, which he tried to replace. Now I understood the guilt behind the gesture. And on top of that, we'd been trapped in the motel during the blizzard, but the hardware store was out of anti-freeze, and now the plumbing we used was a ticking time bomb for the next thaw.

Exposing myself was to prove a point to my family and to show Oz I wasn't afraid anymore. All that did was make both our families want to kill me. I made a mess of everything. And Oz hurt me worse than before.

I didn't want to go back inside and face them all, but I couldn't stay out here much longer. My toes were already on the verge of frostbite. Despite my exceptional healing, replacing digits was firmly left for axolotls and the rumored axolotl shifters.

"Darby," Oz whispered. He reached for my cheek with a thumb to swipe away the tears freezing on my skin.

"Oz, I can't." I brushed away his touch.

"Can we talk? Please, Darby."

Sobs worked their way up my throat. I shook my head, unable to speak, and I ran just beyond the front door threshold—the furthest distance I could maintain while finding clothes. I slipped Dad's hideous sweater I'd turned into a dress over my head, avoiding the naked and half-naked bodies of both our families. And Phil. They awkwardly avoided eye contact with each other while emptying out the closet my parents kept stocked for shifting emergencies.

With the families busy, and me avoiding them and their judgmental whispers, I searched for my purse, keys, and coat resting near the Christmas tree. Good thing I hadn't returned Oz's car key.

Heartbroken, embarrassed, and humiliated all over again, I ignored my family, especially my dad, and marched back out of the door. Oz took a few steps toward me, but I held out my palm, blocking his approach. I had no intention of returning to this two-bit small town ever again, and the only thing between me and my final escape was that car. That's all I focused on.

21
Acceptance

Oz

I DIDN'T WANT A thank you. I only wanted Darby to look at me warmly and invite me back inside. But that didn't happen. On the evening of the most magical night of the year, standing in the dark front yard lit only with twinkling Christmas lights and a warm porch light, I was paralyzed with terror.

A gnawing in my half-empty stomach told me this upset Darby fleeing from me was the last image I'd ever have of her, and that I would never see her again. I had no idea why she was upset with me. I'd only admitted the truth, tried to get her to understand. And my efforts were enough to diffuse the dangerous situation, so things could go back to normal.

"Darby, please give me a chance to explain."

"You said enough," she answered without looking at me.

"I only wanted to help." I only wanted *you*...

Darby kept on moving, her limbs jerking with the cold and her not-entirely healed ankle. I wanted to chase after her, but she would only move faster. And the last thing I wanted was to hurt her more.

Darby climbed into the car I bought her, and I tried not to read into that. With no address, no phone number, her taillights faded into the distance.

"You people are messed up," Phil said, shrugging into his coat and walking down the porch steps. "Thanks for the clothes, but I'm out of here."

I didn't give Phil Parker a response because I didn't care. But also, the frosty air stung my lungs, and I couldn't breathe. I gazed at the void, waiting to see signs Darby had changed her mind.

For five years, I'd debated and replayed that moment in the motel when Darby had revealed her shifter side to me, and how I'd reacted terribly. The only solution I imagined was asking her to shift back so I could show her my other form, too. But I was so damned shocked, I couldn't say anything fast enough. Just like she had been, I was embarrassed and ashamed of what I was.

And from the moment I caused her crash, she seemed to hate me. I'd had opportunities to show her the truth, but I'd put it off. I wanted to know if she cared about me before I put myself out there for her. And instead of risking my heart and telling her straight, I was too little, too late. In my defense, if I would've shifted in front of our families and Phil, I would've started a bloodbath. I had to keep everyone safe, but that meant, once again, I didn't do the right thing by Darby. So I lost her all over again.

"Oz, get inside," Harvey called over.

The taillights were long gone, but I couldn't move my feet. I couldn't look away, hoping Darby would realize she'd overreacted too soon, again, and this time she'd return. We both screwed up.

"Oz!"

But I believed in Darby. Any moment now, a pair of headlights would appear. A tugging at my arm broke my concentration. Harvey stood at my side.

"We're going to finish the meal. Lucy insists we stay. There's too much food for only her and Dennis to finish. I wasn't sure it was a great idea, but Jasper agreed, so come on."

I looked back at the dark horizon.

No, she wouldn't return.

Harvey gave me another tug, and I let my feet carry me into the house. Mindlessly, I returned to my seat. My plate, half finished, was cold. So was the conversation. Phil's seat was empty—good riddance. But so was Darby's.

I blinked rapidly and moved my fork onto my plate.

"I had no idea. Did you know? Can you believe she's a deer?" my mom asked no one in particular. All I could think of was this night would haunt my dreams for the rest of my life, and all my mom could think was...scandal. A deer shifter in a wolf family? The outrage. And, of course, *my* mom had to bring up the conversation right in front of the Hansons.

I picked up a roll and swiped around my plate, wishing I could be in that car with Darby—fleeing. I'd go anywhere with her, and now I lost my chance.

"It happens," Mr. Hanson said evenly, which surprised me, because they didn't know before. And they were being quite calm about it now, even as their daughter fled back to the city on Christmas night, devastated.

"How though?" Mom pressed.

I squeezed my fork. It wasn't an accusation. But for those who weren't affected by the socially devastating anomaly, her confusion shrouded what she really thought—Darby didn't belong. So someone screwed up, and that rejection lit a fire in my veins.

"Like a redhead born of a blond and brunette," my dad said, surprising me. "Genetics are weird, honey."

He was right. Why he bothered to learn this intrigued me. Genetics gave us strange animals in the shifter line on very rare occasions, but when someone was born different from their family and the truth was discovered at shifter puberty, the imprinting lie was commonly used to shame the child for being different. The reason I knew—I hadn't imprinted, and I went digging for answers in a safe place where my family wouldn't find out—the internet. I wouldn't be here without those strangers explaining my differences to me. I doubted Darby had that.

"Weird," Mom mumbled.

Mrs. Hanson didn't say anything, likely feeling the undercurrent of scrutiny. Darby's father was unusually quiet.

"But a deer, though?" Mom pressed. "You're all wolves. How does a prey come from a line of predators?"

"It just does, Mom," I said defensively.

"Huh," she said.

We all chewed in tense silence. I wanted this over with as soon as possible so I could get out of here.

"Jasper, you ever hear of something like this?" Mom asked the golden doctor son.

"It's a small town, Mom. I know it's hard to understand. We're a tight-knit community here, so we aren't exposed to many different...things. When I was a resident, I had to be careful, of course, so questions related to the hidden world were avoided entirely. It's possible I had several patients—I mean, statistically, I probably had a few mismatched shifter patients. But I didn't get a chance to discuss whatever was missing in their psyche to imprint on a different animal than the family's line. I mean, no offense, Dad, but I'm more familiar with a variety of medical cases than you are, and I'm inclined to believe there's clearly a mental defect."

"Med school clearly didn't cover shifter puberty," I said sharply. Jasper looked at me, dumbfounded. "There's nothing wrong with her *psyche*. She didn't imprint. She didn't choose. It's genetic."

"You never mentioned you knew so much about shifter lines." Mom gave Mr. Hanson the side-eye as if still not believing Dad's explanation for the genetic fluke. And I didn't answer her question, which would only drag us into a rabbit hole I had no intention of getting trapped in.

"Well, why didn't she tell us sooner?" Mom added. "I mean, she's not a teenager anymore."

I dropped my fork with a clatter. "Maybe she was embarrassed, Mom. Everyone's overreaction tonight proves she was right to be cautious about it. She showed you she was different, and you all turned on her. You almost attacked her. Every one of you should be ashamed of yourselves."

I didn't know if they were ashamed. But they kept their eyes on their plates, even as Mom said, "You can't blame us for our instincts when prey stood before hungry predators."

"That was *Darby*. Not some rando animal in the woods. Are you hearing yourself?" The disgust twisted my face for me.

"What's gotten into you, Oscar? You're not usually so testy," Mom said.

No, I usually wasn't, but tonight, things were different. Tonight, things weren't about me.

"You should've helped me calm Phil down, not join him in a feed," I said, teeth gritted.

"You like her, don't you?" Mom asked. The tone wasn't teasing. It was judgmental.

Mrs. Hanson gave me dirty looks. I wasn't accepted as a human. I wouldn't be accepted for what I was, either. The Martins might be predators like the Hansons, but that didn't make them friends, and the Martin family secret likely had the Hansons steaming with offense.

"You heard that phrase, 'Don't poke the bear'? Right now, it's good advice," I said and bit off a hunk of cold, gravy-coated roll.

"Oh, nonsense. Bobcats aren't bears," Mom said.

"Honey," Dad said with a stern tone. "Leave Oscar out of this."

"Is there something you want to say, Oz?" Mr. Hanson asked.

Since he was offering and this was his house, I took the opportunity. "There is. Regardless of Jasper's medical degree, he's wrong. Darby was born the way she is. Instead of supporting her, you almost attacked her. Now you're questioning her mental health instead of going after her while she's upset, driving alone in the dark. This is exactly why she kept it a secret from you, because she was afraid the people she loved would reject her. And yet, here we are."

Both our families looked down at their plates in shame.

"She wanted to dump off the motel," Mrs. Hanson said, nose in the air.

"And that's your excuse?" I asked, voice rising.

"No, but it set the tone of the evening," Mrs. Hanson continued. She still remained cool with me. I didn't care. I wasn't trying to impress her anymore.

"How so?" I was dying to hear the excuse.

"She spoiled the evening with her intent to damage the family legacy, and then she shocked everyone with her vulgar display. This right here is all her fault."

I made a noise of disgust and stood. "Address, please," I said to Mr. Hanson.

"For what?"

"I need to make sure she's okay, because neither of you give any shit about her. You don't deserve her." I held out my phone, waiting to type in the address. "Give me Darby's apartment in Green Bay. The attorney's office found her. You have her address. Go ahead. I'm ready."

"We're not giving you her address," Mrs. Hanson said, shocked.

"Why not?"

The Hanson matriarch looked at my family and back as if she couldn't imagine her deer daughter with a bobcat. As if I was the threat to Darby's safety. I was shocked the old woman cared at all, but I wouldn't dignify that judgmental bullshit with the truth. She didn't deserve it. None of them did. I pushed away my chair.

"Where are you going?" Mom asked. "The pie hasn't come out yet."

"All you care about is food and appearances, Mom. All of you disgust me. If Darby ever returns home, which I doubt, because of you, I better see perfect behavior, or we're going to have a problem. Understand?"

Gasps of horror and arguments disrupted the table as I collected my coat and left. I knew exactly how Darby felt, and I was proud of her for having the guts to stand up to those monsters. She only wanted their acceptance. They didn't deserve her.

If I had Darby at my side, I'd have the strength to do it, too, but she wasn't coming back, so there was no point in rocking the boat further. Whenever Darby was away, Christmas gatherings were hell. Tonight was no different, and I didn't have a way to change it.

22
Remind Me

Darby

After that disaster, I was thankful for one thing: I'd only bet myself this year's Christmas party was going to be the worst year. But I didn't actually win an extra fifty bucks. Okay, I was thankful for one other thing: after being trapped in an abandoned motel and afterward staying at my parents' house, there was nothing like home. I'd woken up warm and snuggly in my own comfortable bed to the sounds of the neighbors fighting through my thin walls. Ah, civilization.

I smiled as I showered with hot, running water and dressed in what I felt like wearing. With a towel wrapped around my wet hair, I headed for the fridge full of fresh food, and even better—leftovers. Spaghetti topped with canned chili from before I left. I cracked the lid and gave it a whiff. With a shrug, I popped it into the microwave. I was starving. I didn't get to finish my meal last night, and I'd been too distraught to eat after I'd gotten home super late.

I scrunched my towel-wrapped hair while watching my food spin around, thankful for utilities that didn't run on a limited supply of propane. I grabbed the container and headed for my couch when I slipped on an invisible puddle of water from my sink.

Spaghetti with chili went up in the air while I went down. A nasty crunch on my hip sent pain sparking all over again. Only this time, I didn't have Oz to carry me to safety. I didn't want to think about Oz. I didn't want reminders of what had happened. I was happy being home, and I was perfectly safe where I sat, except the puddle was rapidly soaking up my pajamas. With a sigh, the container landed, and absolutely *sprayed* chili and limp noodles all over the kitchen.

Despite how happy I truly was, now I wanted to cry. Why couldn't the management office fix that leak? Why couldn't I do it myself? Screw the security deposit. I climbed to my feet with a wince and grabbed a towel off the stove handle. I tossed it down and soaked up the immediate concern. Then I cleaned up the ridiculous mess, which took far longer than I wanted.

My stomach grumbled.

Chili sauce had a way of finding nooks and crannies that I didn't know existed, and I didn't need enlightenment. But I cleaned it all, miserably scrubbing, wishing I didn't have to do it myself. Wishing during a moment of weakness Oz was here to help. But I didn't need him. I could do anything I wanted all by myself, but it was nice to have him around. Nope. Not going there again.

With more force than needed, I threw the dirty towels into my washing machine. Above the washer and dryer, inside the cabinets, was a basket of tools. The deposit wasn't going to do me much good if there was worse damage from the leak and they blamed me for not reporting it.

But I had...several times.

I kneeled on a pile of clean towels and ducked under the sink. For a flash, I wished Oz could be doing this. Not because I couldn't, of course, but the view was so much better.

He had been wet, half-naked, and the muscles on his chest, back, and arms glistened as they shimmied with his force. I leaned up and hit my head on the sink basin. What did I need again?

Oz.

No. Fix the leak before my ankle was next. I shut off the valve and dried and cleaned the connection. I didn't have pipe flux or any pipe tape, but I had epoxy putty—good enough until a proper repair could be made.

Just like Oz had said.

Damn it, stop! Why did everything have to remind me of him? How could I push him out of my mind? Because that was my real emergency. Not this leak... Fix the leak. Focus. With a grumble, I kneaded together the two compounds until properly mixed, and I squished it along the seam. That was going to do until management got their heads out of their asses.

I exhaled, proud the stupid leak was finally fixed. Now I could move on with my life. Back to the fridge. I had a full carton of eggs. They needed to be used up, and they wouldn't go on a joyride around the kitchen. I whipped half a dozen, trying to ignore the memory of the sound of Oz working in the motel's kitchen. This was *my* kitchen, *my* eggs, and *my* ketchup. When I finished partially cooking them, I loaded them up with the red sauce...

I double checked the floor in front of the sink. I hadn't turned the valve back on, so regardless of the effectiveness of my repair, I wasn't going to spend another hour cleaning those same nooks and crannies.

But I still moved carefully over to the couch with my steaming bowl of eggs and ketchup. I snuggled under my fleece blanket and pulled up a streaming service. Back in the day, cable companies forced their customers to watch whatever they were paid the most to do so. Now I could avoid all those happy, sappy love story Christmas miracle movies.

That was depressing stuff.

No, I found Die Hard. All that was missing was the wine, but it was too early for that, and Shauna. I sent my best friend a text, inviting her.

I'm coming over right now.

I smiled, expecting as much. *Door's unlocked.*

Shauna popped over to my door in minutes, and she dropped next to me on the couch. She was eager and excited to hear all the details, but I didn't want to remember.

"I've got Die Hard. Up for a re-watch?" I asked to steer the conversation.

"What the hell?" Shauna asked.

"What the hell what?" I repeated.

"I've been texting you for days with no answer, honey. The boss has been asking me where you are, because you weren't answering him, either. You went north and vanished. You had me scared shitless. I almost called the cops, but I trusted you knew what you were doing, and I remembered your warning about the lack of a signal up there. But seriously, one more day and I was calling. With the after Christmas returns rush, you're on the schedule this afternoon, and I'm so glad you're here, because I can't go to work if you're not there."

I'd forgotten all about my job. "I better text the boss quick."

Shauna nodded and studied me, bursting to continue talking while I typed. I informed the boss of a family emergency and a lack of basic civilization up north, and I finished up with a deep apology and a promise to never do it again. Tone was hard to convey over text sometimes, but I had a feeling he was angry, but I wasn't fired yet.

"I'm still employed," I told Shauna and read the next reply, "But one more episode like that, and he's going to cut me loose. Well, it's a good thing I already made sure there will be no more family emergencies in my future."

Nothing like eggs and ketchup for breakfast with threats to your livelihood on the side. I shouldn't have been surprised. Ghosting my boss and best friend was unprofessional and rude, respectively. I was thankful Shauna didn't hate me for it.

"Now that all that's settled, ready to watch?" I asked Shauna.

My best friend stared at me in disbelief.

"What?"

"You were supposed to be gone for two days to dispose of a motel. Something went wrong...or very, very right." Shauna grinned. "Girl, what the hell happened?"

23

The Deets

Darby

SHAUNA WAS HUMAN—AS FAR as I knew, but after the explosive confrontation at my parents' house, now my hidden world radar was questionable, if not outright broken. Telling Shauna about my other form wasn't the same as when I'd opened up to Oz. Back then, we had privacy, and if he reacted in the complete opposite as he had, I had family nearby to help me. Now I was on my own, so I couldn't risk blowing my best friend's mind. I didn't know how she'd react, and I had no support from others to help ease her over the shock. In our apartment community, packed with listening ears, I couldn't tell her the truth exactly.

"A hunter chased a deer across the road, and trying to avoid it, I crashed. Since I was away so long, cue lots of family drama, but now I'm happy to be home."

"That explains the new car in parking spot number sixty-four."

"You noticed?"

"Honey, your car was held together with duct tape."

"Only the tears in the seat cushion and the cracks on the dashboard," I added in my defense. Sure, it wasn't much, but it was mine. I worked hard for it, and I bought it. I struggled to maintain it, but that wasn't the point.

Now I drove around in a constant reminder of Oz.

"I didn't think you could afford something like that. No offense," Shauna said. "Your family sure is generous."

I sighed, needing to give fair credit where credit was due. "It was Oz."

Shauna perked up. "The ex? And that's what I'm here for, the deets. Now spill, starting with what you got him."

I could do this—word vomit a story and press play on the movie, but Shauna's orders had the guilt pressing hard. "I...I didn't get him anything."

"Girl?" Oh, Shauna was disappointed in me.

"All the kids are adults in my family. We don't exchange gifts unless someone really wants to gift someone else. No one's allowed to complain."

"Sounds...relaxing, compared to what we see in the store."

"Why do you think I proposed this idea when I was old enough? I'd seen what the holiday shopping spirit really is, and I didn't want to feed that churn for the stockholders."

"Okay. Excused. Now tell me about this Oz."

"We were snowed in together, and the motel was just as shitty as I expected." I never did pawn it off. Huh. "When the weather cleared, we left, and I stayed at my parents' place for the holiday festivities out of obligation. And since you're curious, they sucked."

Shauna was clearly dissatisfied by that answer. "Snowed in together? I want to hear about the kissing, hugging, and *sex*."

"Is that all you care about?"

"It's the beginning of any healthy relationship."

Said the single lady.

Shauna wouldn't let up until I gave her a satisfactory answer. Dialing up the vagueness,

I said, "Has anyone ever kept something from you for so long that when the truth came out, you couldn't forgive it?"

I'd known Oscar Martin most of my life. I thought he was human, and he never told me anything to make me suspect otherwise. My best friend as a teen, who I harbored a massive crush on—leading me to humiliate myself on the cheerleading squad. And to finally tell him how I felt, I mustered the courage to show him my deer side. But when he'd been disgusted with me, my weeks of fear rapidly building, and the constant worry over breaking the rule, and the ever-present indecision of should I or shouldn't I, finally snapped. I fled. For five years I thought I'd spun that human's pretty head of his and made him afraid of me, disgusted with me, insulted by my years of never revealing the truth. That Oz turned out to be a bobcat shifter. A predator like *them*, like my family.

Five years I wallowed in that humiliation, and now I wallowed in it once more. My family hated what I was. I was shameful. I imprinted on a prey species instead of the predator I was supposed to be. While trying to stand up for myself, Oz's family, my family, and Phil wanted to eat me. To kill me for what I was.

"I don't hold grudges," Shauna said. "Life's too short to stew on things. I prefer to hash out everything on the spot. No one runs. No one hides. Clear the air and figure out the problem, and if the problem can't be solved, then it's a case of agreeing to disagree. If it's something that doesn't shatter the earth, we don't discuss it again. But if it's something that cannot be ignored, like blatant favoritism, or a complete disrespect for my feelings, thoughts, or opinions, then the relationship is dead. Not many guys appreciate me digging all the way to the bottom of an issue rather than burying it, so your mileage may vary with my process. So what truth did you discover that made you run back here?"

I didn't think Shauna was calling me a coward. "Oz lied to me about a major foundational...belief. One that I can't get over. We come from families like..." I thought about it. Two sets of eternally warring, opposing enemies, never to reconcile on principal. Only a curtain of civility, and a mutual rule, kept everyone behaving. "The Hatfields and McCoys."

Shauna squinted. "Romeo and Juliet?"

"Maybe. I suppose, but no one dies or goes to prison in either case."

"I don't know much about the feuding families, but why couldn't they just talk out their differences?"

There wasn't much to say. We were what we were, and I could never be part of them. "Some things can't change, Shauna."

"I don't believe that. I believe people choose to change, and they choose to do what's right, regardless of the circumstances. If your families hate each other that much, then talk it out."

"I tried." I'd showed them.

"Maybe Oz's belief isn't what you think. Maybe he's only influenced by his family. Is he a Hatfield or a McCoy in this scenario?"

"It doesn't matter."

"What if he's doing what he thinks is right by his family but not necessarily right by *him*? Catch my drift?"

Oz had been there, never harming a hair on my head, when I showed him my true self the first time. He knew what I was when he'd rescued me from my burning car and replaced it without even asking. The whole time he fired up the propane, gathered wood, fixed us food, fixed the door, and wrapped my ankle...twice, he knew. Oz had ample opportunity to take advantage of his feral side and make a meal out of me, but he had been nothing but gentle. And when our families argued, he'd supported me for who and what I was.

"I don't know," I said, honestly confused.

"Well, tell me about the motel. You said it's a piece of shit, but what happened when you shouted, 'free motel'?"

"They all said 'thanks, but no thanks.'"

Shauna cringed. "That bad?"

I felt the need to defend the place. "It needs work. Plumbing is a mess. The whole place needs to be updated about fifty years, but the location is great for travelers, and it's the perfect place for holiday parties. I told them it was free, explicitly, and still...crickets."

"That doesn't sound so bad. I wouldn't mind painting walls and hanging art. Sucks living in an apartment forever. But I'd still hire a plumber." Shauna smiled. "So now what?"

"I don't know." I couldn't afford to fix it up myself, not that I wanted to, and no one else who qualified wanted it. "But I think some Die Hard is in order."

Shauna craned her neck toward the microwave clock. "We can watch it once through before our shift starts."

"I'll take it."

I'd been looking forward to hanging out with Shauna since I'd left. I woke the TV and played the movie. After that chat—the parts of it she didn't get—a small twist deep inside had me wishing Oz were here.

24

A Possibility

Darby

I WAS ALREADY ON my boss's bad side, so I convinced Shauna to go to work early. Considering I was driving, she had no problem with that. But for the first time, I parked a little way off to protect my new car from carts and door dents. It was an odd feeling to have something worth preserving and protecting.

"You gonna make me walk that far? There's lots of open spaces," Shauna protested.

Remembering Oz's line when he'd carried me, I said with a nostalgic smile, "You have strong legs."

Shauna rolled her eyes. "Yeah, sure. You just don't want this new baby of yours scratched."

"True."

"I wish I could find a man who would gift me a new car. This guy sounds perfect. Whatever that belief he has, this deal-breaker, must be good."

After the Martins revealed their bobcat side, our families would never get along again. I'd embarrassed and shamed my family publicly. I truly feared the next time I went home, the feral side of my family might just have themselves venison for dinner.

That was enough thinking of home for one day. I had customers to face who wanted returns for cash or store credit. Like every year, this was going to be draining. The store I worked at had been closed for Christmas day, and that was for the better. With Shauna at my side, I pushed through the employee door, and we split up toward our lockers.

"Darby," my boss said, headed straight for me. He was taller than average with rimless glasses. Half the time I didn't notice them at all until the light reflected off them. But his hawk eyes beneath were always watching. So despite his pleasant tone, a knot formed in my stomach.

"Good afternoon, sir. Like I said, I'm sorry about the emergency. I couldn't get a signal up in Powers."

"I'm familiar with the area. My wife and I head out to the casino a couple weekends a month. The lack of cell service is one of the reasons why we go that way."

I nodded, grateful he actually understood. "What can I do for you?"

"I'm glad you're early today. We don't want to conduct business during your shift."

I thinly smiled. Of course not. I'd rather use my personal time, too.

"You weren't around when the bonuses were distributed. Here's yours. Merry Christmas." The boss held out a plain white envelope, and I accepted it, completely surprised.

"Thanks."

"Just between you and me, there's going to be a management position opening soon, and I think you'll be the perfect fit. The team respects you, and I've been told you've been responsible for minimizing labor. That's exactly the kind of attitude we look for." The boss grinned. "I hope you'll consider applying, but this recommendation means you can't have a repeat of last week."

"I told you it'll never happen again, and I mean it."

"Excellent." The boss left, and I pulled open the envelope flap. The first thing I saw was a gift card for ten dollars off a minimum-weight purchase of a turkey or a ham.

I had to force myself not to roll my eyes. Had he seen the prices of meat lately? I thumbed to the paper behind it, a check. From the corporate headquarters, addressed to me...

The door behind me opened, and Shauna appeared. "Darby, there you are. Boss has been looking for you..." Shauna trailed off when she saw my envelope. "Got your Christmas bonus?"

"A hundred bucks could get me two cans of paint."

"Paint?" Shauna repeated, and then her eyes widened. "Are you considering...?"

"No." I had to shut that idea down. I couldn't take over the motel. This was literally enough for some paint. This couldn't reopen or sustain a motel. Besides, I'd already figured out a few reasons why I couldn't return to Powers ever again. Nope, nope, nope.

But if I let myself picture it... A lit Christmas tree, a cozy fireplace, new hardwood floors, classy rugs, warm humming from the new furnace, a full propane tank...

And Oz. Holding a cup of coffee and smiling at me, congratulating me on the hard work paying off. On *our* work paying off.

And a bunch of guests pouring in from a winter's storm to spend a vacation cross-country skiing. Stupid daydreams.

"Whatever magic that motel used to possess died of old age, and now you want to stay here with me. I think Mr. Schreiber is going to return that carpet washer, and he's going to argue it came that dirty," Shauna said.

We stood alone in the run-down employee breakroom, wearing our lovely uniform smocks. I'd spend half the day being yelled at, because the customers forgot their gift receipts, or they lost their return receipts. Daydreams weren't real. This was real. A possibility of a promotion and maybe a raise. That was real.

So was the red car in the parking lot.

Shauna said softly, "He must be really special."

I snorted to myself. "Daydreams are fun, but they aren't reality."

"Why not?"

I frowned. "I can't fix that motel."

"As I said, why not?" Shauna repeated. "You fixed the sink, didn't you?"

"Yeah, but... Well, there's my family. They're overbearing..."

"So, put them in their place."

I did. But I didn't stick around to see if they'd listened. "There's so much work to be done on the motel, and this is only a first step, a tiny first step." I looked at the check. It wasn't much, almost not worth mentioning.

"You're handy. Do the work slowly and have someone help you."

But Oz was there. "I can't see *him* anymore."

"The ex-not-an-ex hot guy? Tell me what this incompatible foundational belief is. Is he Mormon?"

The look on her face made me chuckle. Then I told her the truth. "Apparently, lying by omission is forgivable."

"What was his reason?"

I stared at her in disbelief, mouth gaped open. I didn't stick around long enough to find that out, either. I'd...vanished. I'd cut out on

Oz too early before. Had I done it again? Did I screw up again? "I don't know."

Shauna snorted as if she'd solved the problem. "After you ask him what it was, which I'm sure is good, then you can forgive him."

I'd lied by omission, too, but I had a good reason. But then Oz knew what I was, so what could possibly be a good reason for not showing me his bobcat side? For the first time, I was curious.

I looked at my best friend. Every word out of her mouth was encouraging me to go. "Why do you want me to leave you, Shauna?"

Shauna gripped my upper arms. "You think I dreamed of working here when I was a little girl? If something better comes along, I'll take it, and if that means I have to leave the city, I'll go. Darby, I love you, but when there's a chance at real happiness, don't let it slip away. I keep my eyes peeled all the time, and I see you're covering yours."

Shauna walked away, heading to punch in, as if she didn't want me to argue about that.

25

The Choice

Darby

I WAS EXHAUSTED. I couldn't think straight anymore. All week, I'd come home on tired feet with sweat-stained clothes. The week after Christmas was always rough, and each night was no exception. I'd tried to sleep, but it wouldn't be within grasp. Eventually, I'd tossed and turned enough I forgot if I was still awake. And when the sun rose, I'd squint and get up. Then I'd shuffle out to the kitchen for coffee. The reason for lack of sleep? All week, I'd thought of nothing, but the conundrum Shauna had trapped in my head.

To stay or to go. Each had its merits. This morning I did the routine shuffle to the kitchen, and while the drip machine burbled, I checked the leak under the sink. It was dry.

I smiled, proud of my handiwork. Then again, I could fix just about anything.

With a strong cup of brew warming my veins, I sat on the couch. The boss had recommended me for a promotion. He hadn't specified when, and he hadn't divulged if there would be a raise. Considering how precarious my standing was with attendance, I hadn't pressed. But getting away from the registers and the customer service desk and being allowed to make my own schedule—within reason—was appealing.

As of right now, I was on the naughty list, and all my vacation requests for the next several weeks were denied. So I had to make tonight count—New Year's Eve. I didn't have any plans.

I knew what Shauna would say. Returning to Oz and asking him why he didn't tell me he was a bobcat was very tempting, and for the record, Shauna voted for this option. I did tell Shauna about the promotion, and her argument had been predictable. *There is no promotion until it's in writing.* Technically, she was right, but if I couldn't get back from no-cell-phone-land for my shift tomorrow, I'd lose my job.

But if I stayed the good employee, brown-nosing for a promotion that might never come, I'd disappoint Shauna. More importantly, every day I'd think about Oz, wondering about the answers to the questions building up. I couldn't escape my own thoughts. I drove the greatest gift anyone had ever given me.

A car. Seriously.

Even though he claimed he'd wrecked mine, I didn't deserve what he'd picked for me. The luxury had to be from a lack of options.

I checked under the sink once more, and still no leaks. A flash of Oz under the motel's kitchen sink returned, only this time, both of us were there, fixing it together. He'd still be half naked, but I'd be wearing a shirt, just in case vendors or suppliers arrived, or family came to help unexpectedly.

I made a snort of disbelief. Those damned daydreams.

I curled up on the couch and sipped. Shauna and I didn't get to finish the movie last week, and I'd been too tired to bother, so I played it. John McClane only wanted a second chance with his wife, who'd moved away for a better career. After he saved her life, and those of most of her company, she realized what was more important. I'd seen this movie, the greatest Christmas movie ever, more times than I could count, but this was the first time it made me cry. The choice was there, waiting for me. A life-changing choice that could make my daydreams come true or end up with me right back here, hanging with John McClane and Shauna while scrolling the job ads. One possibility ended with something just like where I was now, but probably worse.

Only one of those options ended with a possibility of happiness. I had to find out the reason why Oz didn't tell me he was a bobcat shifter, or I was never going to sleep well again.

Darby

WHEN I REACHED THE edge of the snowy but sunny village, I pulled out my phone and searched for a signal. Nana and Gramps had always hosted a New Year's Eve party at the motel, but like the holiday party this year, it was likely at my parents' house. The line rang, and Mom answered.

"Darby? Is that you?" Music pumped through the line, and I could hear laughter. They were having a blast, and I was about to throw a wrench into the gears. Or more accurately, crack a pipe and spring a leak. Did they deserve that? Should I just leave well enough alone?

A knot formed in my stomach.

"Darby? I can't hear you. If you can hear me, the party is at our house. Please come." The line went dead.

My brows lifted. I was invited? After everything that happened, they wanted *me* there? What the hell happened while I was gone?

I tossed my phone onto the passenger seat and gripped the wheel, navigating carefully on the roads. They were still snowy, but the snow was packed hard, and where the sun had hit, areas melted and refroze into ice. Thankfully, Oz wasn't out chasing another poor deer because I didn't see one anywhere, and when I approached my parents' house, the line of cars was telling. Oz's Jeep was here.

My stomach fluttered with nerves. This was going to be so awkward, but I had to do it. I had to face them all and get answers. I had to channel my inner John McClane, without the guns, blood, and dead thieves—so only the good parts. I parked and climbed out, ankle fully healed. But I was still careful. Nothing could derail me from getting that answer.

I didn't bother knocking on the door. No one would hear me. Lifting my chin high, I pushed my way inside. Everyone wore pretty sweaters, khakis or dark jeans, and almost everyone had headbands with sparkly doodads on top. As people turned to see the newest arrival, they quieted and stared. Oz was chatting with his brother, Jasper, and when the quiet reached them, they turned to face me, too. Oz's face reminded me of exactly the reaction he'd had when I showed him my deer. Shock, confusion, and what I'd missed before—relief. This time, I wasn't running away.

"I need answers," I said loudly, staring right at Oz. His sparkly headband had the new year in puffy balloons on top.

Everyone faced him. Oz handed his drink to Jasper and said to me, "You'll get them." He headed straight for the couch for a blanket, and then he bent under the Christmas tree. We all watched. As he approached me, he held out the folded blanket with a brightly wrapped small gift, no bigger than the palm of my hand, on top—the one he'd given me for Christmas, but I'd never opened it.

"I don't want presents. I need answers," I insisted.

"Humor me, okay?" Oz's bright green eyes almost glowed with excitement.

We were in this mess because I hadn't given him a chance to explain before, so I accepted the stack.

Oz smiled, sending my heart fluttering, and he tossed his silly headband on the couch. "Now follow me." He rose his voice, "If everyone could follow me, right out front, I'd appreciate it."

Now I was really confused. Others spilled out, and I checked their faces for any sign they knew what was going on, but they appeared just as puzzled as I was. I exited with our families, unexplainable stack in my hands.

Oz stood in the front yard and gestured for me to stand by his side. Our families looked expectantly at me, so I did. I'd half expected snarky comments or rude mumbles, but so far, nothing. It was beyond weird.

"Remember what we discussed," Oz said to the onlookers.

Once again, our families looked at each other, trying to figure out what Oz meant. And with that, Oz was glimmering with excitement. He said quietly to me, "I've wanted this chance since the crash, and I kept screwing up again and again. I lost the opportunity to set things straight, and now I'm not going to make any mistakes. While you were gone, I had a chat with our families. They don't know what I'm going to show you, but I can assure you, nothing bad will happen. You're safe. We both are."

Both of us? "Oz, I don't know what to say."

"Just watch."

Oz stripped off most of his clothes, and yes, as a dutiful friend—or hopefully something more—I watched. I memorized. I admired his full body covered in nothing but boxers and socks, with beautiful blond chest hair and amazingly sculpted muscles. His nipples instantly hardened, and I bit my lip to hide my grin. Oz shifted in front of everyone.

I thought our families gasped and murmured, but I wasn't paying any attention to them. I was frozen, baffled...relieved. All these things flooded me so quickly I didn't understand. Pieces of our past connected. Each confusion became clear. Each comment made sense. Everything was right.

Oz was a deer.

I covered my mouth with my hands, admiring the twelve-point buck with a twenty inch spread. Oz nuzzled my shoulder. Tears sprung to my eyes, and I blinked them away. I couldn't let anything interfere with this...this magnificence before me.

Oscar Martin was beautiful.

After he gave me a quick noise, I tossed the blanket over his broad shoulders, and he shifted back. I held the sides tight to keep him warm and snorted back my tears. "Why didn't you tell me?"

"For the same reason you never told your family, I never told mine." He gestured with his head to indicate the Martins watching us, completely shocked like me. "And now I need you to open that gift."

At least they didn't shift to attack, and I was thankful for that.

"But Oz…"

"Open the gift." An uncovered finger pointed at the palm sized gift remaining in my hand. "You forgot that when you fled. I hoped you would've taken it, but since you didn't, I wished you'd return so you could open it, because it's important."

I opened the beautifully wrapped gift and found a jewelry box.

"Go ahead," Oz pressed.

I opened the lid and found a locket. "What is this?"

"Open it." Oz was smiling, eager for me to finish figuring out what this puzzle meant.

26
Open It

Darby

I LIFTED OUT THE locket, which made a noise, like something was broken inside. I carefully popped open the lid, so I didn't lose any parts, and what I found was an entirely new puzzle. Dark gray little balls. "Are these diamonds that haven't been cut?"

Oz chuckled. "Nope."

"They're so perfectly round. Like pellets..."

"Closer."

"From a shotgun? You know I hate hunting."

Oz nodded, amused at my slowly twisting gears.

"You put the spent pellets from a shotgun shell in a locket. Why?"

From the outside of the blanket, Oz tapped his hip.

I gasped and dropped the locket and the pellets. My hands moved to my gaped mouth. I couldn't believe it. All this time. Oz's passionate speech about my hunting—or lack thereof. He'd known. He *had* been there.

"I shot you!"

Oz grinned.

"Oh, my god. I shot you? Oz, you never told me. Oh, my god. I'm so sorry. Does it hurt?"

His beautiful smile moved with his words. "We were teens when it happened. I was healed after a week."

"You were the poor deer I hunted, and you were the idiot deer in the road. Always there," I said in admiration. "You saved my life when I'd crashed, but I saved yours...twice."

"And I never forgot."

"I can't believe this."

"Darby," Oz lowered my hands with his, still holding the blanket. He had to be cold by now, but he didn't show it. "I've always watched over you. Sometimes, I got a little too close." He laughed, and I copied him, but my laughter was coated with tears. "You were my best friend all those years, and I've always admired your strength, because I wasn't as strong as you. When I discovered what I was, I was terrified of how you'd react, just like you were of me. But when you showed me your deer side five years ago, I was speechless, shocked with happiness. When you left, you took my heart with you."

Our families murmured and whispered along the porch. Some stood in the front yard, but everyone watched intently. Oz showed no sign of being shy anymore.

"My entire memory has you in it, and I don't want any memories without you," Oz continued. "I've waited for you to return all this time, and I'd continue to wait forever for you, because you're worth it to me. You are everything to me. I love you, Darby Hanson."

I snorted a wet laugh, completely thrown by Oz finally pouring his heart out to me. "I've waited forever for you to say that. I love you, Oz. I think I have since we were kids. I joined the cheerleading squad because of you."

Oz cringed. "Sorry. I was an ass sometimes, but I liked looking at yours in that outfit."

I smacked him on the arm playfully, since I liked looking at his while he was under the sink.

Oz squeezed my hands in his. "But if you feel like the city is where you're meant to be, I'll follow you."

Tears flooded my eyes again. "You'd move to the city just for me?"

"I'd follow you anywhere. I'm lost without you."

I grinned. I couldn't imagine myself anywhere but with Oz at my side, and now I knew exactly what I had to do, what I was called for. What Nana would be proud of. "Then that's settled. We're staying here. Impending plumbing from hell, but we can fix it together."

"The motel was winterized," Oz said.

"It was, until we used it, remember?" I countered.

"I bought all the anti-freeze and winterized it while you were getting your ankle looked at. You're welcome."

That's why he'd dropped me off. While his brother tended to my injury properly, Oz tended to the motel properly. "*You* did! I went to the hardware store. They were sold out."

Oz grinned. He'd always been looking out for me.

"Before we get back into that exciting project, I have one thing left to do," Oz said, a big grin still on his face. I liked this Oz. The cheeriness and lightness of having no burdens suited him. He opened his blanket wide and captured me inside it. His arms pressed me against that sexy body of his. And now I knew why he wasn't cold. In here was toasty warm. And so very naked. I wanted to back up and take a much needed and long awaited gaze, but I'd settle for exploring with my hands.

Those pale eyes of his almost glowed. Now I realized they did glow when his shifter side had been emotional, it popped out. I'd never caught it before, and now his eyes glowed yellow, even against the bright sunlight. His angular mouth found mine, and he held me in place, a firm surprise telling me exactly how much he wanted me right now. I was thankful for the blanket. Oz's kiss was better than the last time. Before, it was a celebratory peck on the lips because we were free, and quickly he'd switched into a sensuous kiss, as if it would be our first and last at the same time. An exploration and a goodbye all at once.

This time, Oz's kiss was like the first of many. Excitement permeated his whole hard, fluctuating body. As his lips took mine, my hands memorized all those ridges and felt those movements while he pulled me closer. But I couldn't get close enough. I wanted to grab what else became hard, but we had an audience. I settled for raking my hands through his floppy blond hair, pinning his face near mine.

Oz didn't want to wait for the New Year to ring in, and I was glad. I was tired of waiting. I wanted Oz today, and I wanted him forever.

This wasn't an end. This was our beginning.

And I loved it.

27

The Best Memory

Oz

I'VE WAITED WAY TOO many years to have Darby in my arms. I'd daydreamed of this moment for years, imagining how it would go, what I would do, and in what order I would do it in. All that fretting about being perfect was for nothing. The rest of the world faded away. All my thoughts and worries vanished.

I picked up Darby, just as I'd carried her when I hurt her ankle and freed her from the burning car. And I carried her toward my modest house. It was one story, built in the fifties, but I fixed and updated it over the years. It wasn't much, but I was proud of it.

There was one thing about Darby and her strength that I was curious about. "Darby, after all those years, why did you show your family your deer that night?"

Darby's arms were around my shoulders, and they gave me a strength I'd never known before. "Because they insulted you, and I couldn't live with it. They held you back from college. They treated you like a misfit. I decided that was my breaking point, but I understand why you tolerated it as long as you did. We're both the same in so many ways."

But not related. I looked that up immediately after Darby showed me her deer five years ago.

"They didn't hold me back. I had a college fund. I chose to stay here."

"Why? There's nothing here, or there wasn't."

"I waited for you to return."

Darby faced me, and I set her down in my living room. "Oz..."

"If I left, I didn't know when I'd see you again. I couldn't risk losing you again, so I waited."

"That's sweet, but now I feel guilty."

"Why?"

"Because you could've done anything with your life. You're smart, Oz. You could've been anything. You could've done more than Jasper."

She called me a genius and a lazy bum all in one. I smiled. "I didn't want anything but to give you the best life I could. So, to me, that meant being here. I'm happily self-employed. I have this great house, and I bought you a car without a second thought. I can give you what you need, even if that's a hammer, a can of paint, or a bunch of anti-freeze. The moment you say so, I can get that propane tank refilled."

Darby's eyes glimmered once more. "You're perfect. You know that, right?"

I had to lean into that one. "Of course, I am. Now you get to experience the perfection that waited for you."

Darby lifted a beautiful, dark brow. "Oh? I like the idea of experiencing perfection. What exactly did you have in mind?"

"I'm going to slowly strip you naked."

Darby grinned. "Uh, huh. And then what?"

My hands rested on her hips as I walked her in the right direction toward my bedroom. "I have to keep you warm on this chilly January evening, so I'm going to kiss every inch of skin on your body."

I slipped her shirt over her head and started kissing her shoulders. Heat rushed to my cock, but I had to remind myself to take my time. Darby deserved perfection, and if I let in the magnitude of this event, I was going to explode all over myself.

She stopped. "Is it this one?"

"Nope. Keep going." I planted another kiss on her shoulder.

"This place isn't that big."

"Other things are."

Darby chuckled, and I unfastened the bra hooks resting against her smooth back, which was a surprisingly difficult task while we both walked.

"Left turn."

Darby turned to face me at the threshold. "Now it's my turn."

"You're only half naked," I protested.

"So *you* should be half naked, too," Darby countered and bit her lip.

"Fair enough." I lifted the hem of my T-shirt and flung it aside.

Darby gazed at my chest, and I tightened my pecs for her. She frowned in disapproval, so I gave her a pec pump, and she fought a smile. "That was too fast."

"I can put my shirt back on and go much slower."

"Nah. I want to see the rest, this time without an audience."

I picked up Darby by the hips, and she wrapped her legs around me. I carried her to my bed and leaned over, gently resting her on top.

Darby released me, and I straightened to unbutton my jeans. Darby watched, grinning and biting her lip, as if trying to hide how much she enjoyed this. I loved that she enjoyed this.

Enjoyed *me*.

Learning from my T-shirt failure, I slowly stripped off my jeans while rocking my hips, giving her my best stripper impersonation, until I was wearing nothing but my boxers, which were telling.

"Are you going to strip me, or do you want to watch?" she asked.

"Lady's preference."

Since I'd already unhooked her bra, she tossed it over, freeing her generous breasts. With a lift of her hips, she unfastened her jeans and slid them down. "The rest is all yours."

My turn to smile. "That's fair."

I leaned over her, eager to tear off the remaining scrap of fabric between us and pound into her like I'd dreamed as a teenager. I was far more mature now. More in control. More patient.

And I was going to hear her scream my name.

At least twice.

I stretched up and over her. Darby pressed me down against her as if eager to feel what lie ahead. I didn't mind. My cock was hers and hers alone.

I kissed her earlobes one after the other, and Darby gasped. Her hands palmed my ass and squeezed, and I groaned and collected myself. I had to make Darby's night the one—The One—worth remembering forever. Refocusing on her, I kissed her throat, from ear to clavicle on each side. Darby groaned, and her breaths quickened.

Her hands reached up my back and pressed against the muscle holding me above her, so I lowered myself. The length of my hard cock pressed against her clit, and I rocked while I kissed a sensuous trail from her throat to her left breast. Darby arched under me, and

I found a nipple with the flick of my tongue. Darby gasped again and moaned. My cock throbbed, begging for entrance.

I wasn't biased against any part of a woman's body, so I gave her other breast the attention it equally deserved. And while I spent time unraveling the tension in her body, I dragged my fingers along her sensitive inner thigh. When I found her apex, my fingers swapped place with my cock. I explored deep inside her.

Darby gasped. Her hips moved as if of their own volition, so I helped her. My fingers slid in and out, and I wetted my thumb before finding that sensitive, firm clit of hers. Focusing on her movements, I stroked evenly, not too close, not too far away. I didn't want to overwhelm her with the sensation. With a seemingly endless source of stamina, I kept kissing and stroking. I wanted to worship every inch of her skin, but I focused on the places that mattered most.

Darby's hands gripped fistfuls of my bedding, and her breaths became quick. I lifted away from her beautiful breasts to give her teases at her throat. Her breathing hitched in little stops and starts, and at once, she held her breath. Every muscle in her body tensed. There it was.

She screamed my name and climaxed on my fingers. That scream, the heaves of those breasts—I almost shot my load right then and there. "*You* calling my name is the sexiest thing I've ever heard, but we're not done yet."

Darby smiled. "Is that a promise?"

"Yes, ma'am."

"Then how about you take those boxers off and fill me up proper?"

I groaned. "Now *that's* the sexiest thing I've ever heard." And I never freed myself from my boxers so fast in my life. I lowered myself back onto Darby and repeated the sensuous kisses. Her hips rocked, anticipating my penetration, and I used a hand to guide my length to her eager opening. I'd planned on sheathing myself in slowly, but she was slick.

I slipped against those tight muscles, gliding fully inside in only a few thrusts. Then I stopped. I wrapped an arm under her hips and fastened myself into her, refusing to let her move.

"Everything okay?" she asked, worried.

"More than okay."

After a beat, I released my grip on her and began moving in and out, each stroke faster than the last, and I rose up and watched her breasts bounce. Darby's legs fastened over my hips, and she arched with me, meeting my thrusts.

With my cock inside Darby, I couldn't make it last. I'd dreamed about this moment for too long. I'd built it up to where the overwhelming excitement and anticipation were too much. "Come with me," I ordered, my fingers sliding down to her clit once more.

"I'm almost there."

"Me too." I wished I could come more than once. Women were lucky that way. The more and more I thrust, the heat and warmth flowed, hardening my cock, building the orgasm on the edge of crashing over. "Come with me, Darby. Come now. I can't hold out. I'm going to fill you up completely."

Darby panted. "I'm...I'm..."

"Right now," I called. "Right now. I'm coming for you."

"I'm coming!" Darby shouted.

I blasted into her. The orgasm rushed through me and pulsated on and on, but I locked myself firmly against her hips while

I panted. Sweat poured down my chest, and Darby stroked it with a satisfied grin on her face like I'd never seen before.

I lowered myself once more and kissed her gorgeous mouth. "Was that worth the wait?"

"That was the best I've ever had, but I didn't get to do anything," Darby said.

"You being here is enough for me, but if it makes you feel better, you can do whatever you want to me next time."

"Next time?" Darby asked playfully. "Awfully confident, I think."

"If there's anything you didn't like, I'm more than happy to practice again, and again, and again." Darby laughed. When she settled, I got serious. "I want to get it right for you, Darby. I want to be your last, and I don't want you to have any regrets."

"What are you saying?"

"I kept my promise to keep your secret from your family. I want a promise from you."

"That's fair."

"Marry me," I said in a breathy whisper.

"Oz—" Darby started and for that moment, my heart stopped. Was I too soon? For me, I'd already waited an eternity. But it wasn't for her. Did I chase her off? Was this another in the long line of mistakes I'd made? Would I regret this night forever? My mind continued to spin while Darby's half a second pause felt like minutes. "I would love to marry you."

My lips found hers, and I fell onto her, unable to get physically close enough. I could never get enough of Darby Hanson.

I pulled back for a second and stroked the sweaty hair away from her face.

"That wasn't a fair promise exchange," Darby said.

"Are you having regrets already?" I plucked a lock of wet hair from her forehead and settled it back on the pillow. My hands cupped the sides of her face, and since I'd never gotten this close for this long, I memorized every line on her face. Every curve in her nose. Every lash on her lids.

"Not at all. I just wanted to point that out. I love you, Oz."

"I know right now this is the best memory I will ever have. You made that possible, Darby. I love you more than I can properly convey."

Darby chuckled. "I think I have some idea."

28
Epilogue

Darby

RIGHT AFTER BEING ENCOURAGED to take an upcoming promotion, I'd broken the only rule my boss gave me. Well, after that amazing New Year's Eve with Oz, I wasn't getting to work on time even if I wanted to. So when I'd been presentable, I borrowed Oz's Jeep and my parents' ancient landline, and I'd called to quit. My boss had been upset I gave no notice, especially after that generous hundred-dollar bonus and holiday meat coupon. I called Shauna next. Wait until the boss finds out I stole one of his favorite employees on my way out. I hung up, not feeling the slightest bit guilty.

But Dad sure looked the part. He approached, demeanor soft. "I ain't the most observant man, kiddo, and since you never showed us your natural form, I assumed you were just like us. But now I understand why you never wanted to go hunting. It ain't in your DNA. I'm sorry for not figuring out you were different."

That wasn't good enough. "Oz is different. I'm different. Shifters or not, all of us are different in our own ways, Dad. There's no excuse to treat others so terribly. Just because it's me, and you apologized, doesn't make it okay."

"I understand. I'll do better, Darby."

I knew all those years of prejudice ingrained in his psyche would take time to unravel, but that was a start. The doorbell rang, and I answered it.

A trio of men I didn't recognize stood on the doorstep wearing suits and serious gazes.

I knew almost everyone in the village area, but I gave the rehearsed speech to these strangers, anyway. "We are confident in our beliefs, and we don't need any bibles, thanks." I started closing the door, but a hand stopped me. I had to upgrade to the next level of avoidance. "We're apostates and proud of it."

That didn't work either. "Mormons?"

Still nothing.

The suited stranger in the middle said, "We received a report of possible human exposure to the hidden world. We're here to fix the problem."

My brows lifted. "Fix it how? Are you like an emergency vampire response team, who compels humans, or memory demons?"

"More or less," the left one said. They all looked identical, like an organized military outfit or something. Interesting, but irrelevant in the end.

"Well, we're all shifters, so you're out of luck. Thanks for dropping by."

The trio exchanged confused glances. A tinny alarm came from the wrist of the Super on the right. He glanced at it and said, "Andras has another task for us. Let's go."

They turned and walked down the steps while I closed the door. Brows raised, I wanted to ask what the consequences were for the perpetrator of the exposure, but that would've been too suspicious.

Yikes.

I wondered who called them? Probably Phil. That wolf shifter wasn't worth another thought. Because I had my deer to get home to.

Darby

Oz had enough funds available to get the Magic Powers Motel back up and running, so together we crafted a budget, rolled up our sleeves, and with extra help—namely Riggs, Rusty, Shauna, and Harvey, we were able to make Nana proud.

After a few months, my dad arrived with his tail between his legs, hoping for forgiveness. I wanted our family close again. I craved that love I'd missed for so long, and because of that, I'd offered him a hammer.

Dad had lit up and then exclaimed Mom was bringing food to feed us all. The gravy had been lumpy. When I'd told her politely, she invited Oz to be the official gravy keeper, and Dad didn't say a word about it. That was progress in the best way.

We even started up a shuttle going to and from Riggs's bar, and Shauna turned out to be great at marketing. With the group effort, we booked most of the rooms solid for months. And now there was only one thing missing—the annual Christmas party, just like Nana and Gramps used to host. Everyone was invited.

Except Phil.

I sipped from the celebratory champagne. A fire crackled in the fireplace, and I'd cleaned up the photos Nana had left behind. Now they sparkled. And there were new ones—namely Oz and I laughing together, dusty, paint splattered, and sometimes wet from plumbing issues.

Christmas music streamed throughout the lobby, a gentle background to the murmurs of the packed crowd. Icicle string lights draped around the lobby, flickering in a pattern, as if real icicles were melting. That was Shauna's idea. And the main draw was the towering Christmas tree—not from Phil's farm—wrapped in white lights only. Shauna's request had been easy to grant. The hardwood floors glinted with the sparkling lights. Guests drank and laughed, standing around the lobby or filling the oversized couches—new ones.

It was as magical as the motel used to be, but somehow even better.

"Hey, Darby," Dad said, approaching with a half a glass of champagne. "Not bad. Not bad at all. Oz was right about you."

"Me? What did he say this time?" I darted a smile at Oz, who was a gracious host to his less-than-gracious parents. Eventually, they came around to the idea of their bobcat line having a deer in it.

"He said whatever you put your mind to always turns out perfect. I didn't believe him at the time, but I sure do now."

That was the best compliment I was going to get. I took it. "Thanks, Dad."

"He said you fixed the plumbing. That true?"

"I did."

Dad smiled proudly. "Huh." We stood and sipped for a beat. "Do you think your kids will be deer or wolves?"

"Dad!" I slapped him on the shoulder, embarrassed. Oz and I hadn't announced our engagement yet, since we wanted everyone focused on the motel and not on wedding preparations. I could marry Oz at the courthouse wearing a burlap sack and sporting the worst case of the flu, and I wouldn't care. I only wanted him.

"They could be bobcats," he added, "but Mr. Martin tells me wolves are the more dominant species. Of course they are."

"Seriously, stop it." They'd been talking about this behind our backs. I didn't know if I loved that support, or if I was too embarrassed to want to think about it.

Dad chuckled and rested a hand on my shoulder. "I'm proud of you, Darby. And, I'll admit, I'm glad you didn't kill that deer."

I snorted. "Me too."

"Everything looks great." Dad sipped, gazing at Shauna's decor.

Mom stuck her head out of the kitchen. "Darby, get Oz in here. I need a hand."

Even though the party had returned to its home base, Mom insisted on making a meal for as many as she could, as if she felt the need to participate in her own way. I gestured to her that I'd heard, excused myself from Dad, and moved through the crowd to the best man I'd ever known. "Oz, Mom needs you in the kitchen."

"Does she now?" Oz raised a brow with a grin and gave me a kiss on the cheek. He handed off his champagne to me and disappeared into the kitchen. I finished off both our glasses and brought them to the bar for Shauna to clean.

His gravy really was the best, but I didn't think Mom was making a full spread. We only had room for a standing buffet.

The lights dimmed, and the music quieted. I turned, confused, and all the guests and our families were moving away. Dad and Mr. and Mrs. Martin went into the kitchen.

"What happened? Something went wrong, and they don't want to tell me," I said, half to myself and half to Shauna. I had to know, and I had to fix it. This was Nana's motel, and I couldn't let her legacy die.

"It's probably nothing," Shauna said, but it wasn't reassuring.

I started moving toward the kitchen when Oz reappeared. Our families and guests gave us space. Many of them smiled. Shauna was swiping tears out of her eyes.

"What's going on?" I whispered, expecting some kind of grand reopening speech—that no one bothered to tell me about.

Oz took my hand and spoke loud enough for everyone to hear. "Darby, this motel is filled with wonderful memories and wonderful people from our childhoods on up. We thought this place was lost when Nana and Gramps Hanson moved on from it. But you returned and poured your heart into this place. You revived our histories, our homes, and our hearts. And that love is all around you. That love is here beside you." Oz faced me, hands firmly in mine. "Darby, you tried to take my life once, but it was always yours, and I couldn't imagine the rest of my life without you in it."

Tears glistened in my eyes, and I let out a small laugh, remembering the shot he'd gifted me in a locket I still wore around my neck. But I'd packed it with cotton, so it didn't rattle all the time.

Oz gestured. I turned to find my parents side by side with his parents, walking in their animal forms. Strapped to my mother's back was a flowery pillow and on top, a sparkling ring.

"Oz, there are humans here," I whispered, remembering the trio I didn't want to see again.

"A vampire owed me a favor. He compelled them to forget any mentions or sightings of animals and any nudity."

I'd already agreed to marry him, but this show, this display in front of everyone, was sweet and more than I ever expected. Oz lifted the ring off the pillow and dropped down to one knee. "Darby Hanson, will you marry me?"

With wet eyes and a big grin, I nodded enthusiastically and shouted, "Yes!"

Applause and tinkling glass accompanied Oz lifting me up into his arms and giving me a spin. When he lowered me, Oz kissed me. Now whoops and cheers filled the lobby.

This was the kiss that didn't say I missed you or I dreamed about what this would be like forever. This kiss didn't say I wish things could be different.

This was the kiss that said, 'I love you' and everyone needed to know it. Oz pulled back and slipped the ring on my finger. Under the shimmering Christmas lights, it sparkled a soft ivory and gold.

"It's beautiful. Thank you. This was all...so wonderful."

"The setting was my grandmother's, but the stone has been upgraded."

"You didn't need to do that," I said.

"I wanted to. Darby. I love you so much."

"I love you too, Oz." I only had one regret. "I wish I could've figured everything out sooner. We could've had five more years together."

While the cheers and laughs quieted into refills, and the music resumed its party volume, Oz rubbed my hands. "It's not the quantity but the quality that matters to me. So let's make the next fifty the best years of our lives."

Nana, my stubborn grandmother, had insisted I take over the motel. She'd been far more wise than I'd realized, and now I was truly happy.

All of this was thanks to Nana, that brilliant, sweet, old woman.

Dear Reader,

As an indie author, I'm thrilled you shared your time with me, exploring the crazy worlds and voices living rent-free in my head and keeping me up at night. Your reviews are very important to me, so if you enjoyed this book, please consider leaving some stars at your favorite retailer for Darby and Oz's story, Deer Holiday.

If you found any typos or errors, I blame my cat. Rat her out at: support@stephanieflynn.com.

Thank you for your support!

Also By Stephanie Flynn

Find my catalog at StephanieFlynn.com

Immortal Protector series

0.5 Vampire's Distraction

1 Vampire's Deception

2 Vampire's Secret

3 Vampire's Promise

3.5 Elf Bound

4 Vampire's Demand

5 Vampire's Destruction

6 Vampire's Conquest

Immortal Protector Side Tales

Deer Holiday

Love Claws
Depths of the Heart

Matchmaker in Time series
0.5 Minutes to Live
1 Seconds to Act
2 Hours to Arrive
3 Days to Hide
4 Years to Savor

Pirates in Time series
1 Pirate's Prize
2 Pirate's Treasure
3 Pirate's Plunder

Time Travel Romance Shorts
Fateful Time
One Crazy Time

If you like your urban fantasy without the romance, too, check out Stephanie Flynn's other name, Marie Flynn!

About Stephanie Flynn

Stephanie Flynn writes action-packed paranormal romance filled with adventure, suspense, and danger. She lives in Michigan, USA, with her husband and kids, and she spends her writing time surrounded by a herd of normal cats who bat everything off her desk, including her coffee. Check out her website for more books: StephanieFlynn.com

www.ingramcontent.com/pod-product-compliance
Lightning Source LLC
Chambersburg PA
CBHW030144200726
48285CB00006BA/1935